HARMONY WEST

For every saint searching for his sinner

"No grave can hold my body down. I'll crawl home to her."

— HOZIER

NOTE FROM S.T. NICHOLSON

Dear Reader,

The book you are about to read contains graphic content. This story was written for those who prefer their romance dark and twisted. My muse is my obsession and I will not apologize for the lengths I'll go to make her mine.

Proceed with caution. For more detailed warnings, visit www.harmonywestbooks.com.

Whether you'd like to skip over or skip to the sensual chapters in this book, you can find these scenes in Chapters 2, 3, 4, 7, 9, 13, 14, 16, and 33.

Enjoy, sinner.

– S.T. Nicholson

CHAPTER ONE

BRIAR

IF MY STALKER INSISTS ON HOLDING ME CAPTIVE, I MIGHT as well enjoy my stay at his enormous Gothic estate.

Nicholson Manor is the home of every writer's dreams, secluded deep in the woods on the peaceful mountainside. The vibrant red double doors are the only pop of color on the dark, looming mansion. Giant columns hold up the roof above the entrance, while sunlight pours in through the massive floor-to-ceiling windows, transforming the dark interior of the manor from spooky to opulent. Under the moonlight, Nicholson Manor morphs back into the eerie home perfect for housing the ghosts and ghouls of every writer's disturbed mind.

On the bed beside me is a tray covered with scrambled eggs, bacon, burnt toast coated in a thick layer of peanut butter, and waffles absolutely smothered in syrup. My perfect breakfast. Saint de Haas may be the most skilled stalker to walk the earth.

I'm nearly finished scarfing down every bit of food in sight when he saunters into the room. Saint is already dressed in his usual dark slacks and pressed button-up, sleeves rolled to the elbows. His jet-black hair curls adorably around his ears, his sharp jaw, regal nose, and prominent cheekbones all chiseled from marble. His height is towering and intimidating in a way that makes my mouth water. The curves of muscle along his biceps and shoulders make me long for him to tuck me back into bed, wrap me in his arms, and make me forget the whole world.

"How did you sleep?" he asks in a low, lulling murmur.

The burgundy duvet on his bed is so soft, it should be illegal. The mattress practically molds to my body. And what man owns silk pillowcases? I'm convinced he researched the best pillowcases for a woman's hair and purchased them specifically for my arrival.

"Horribly," I snipe. "Your body heat made me sweat all night. You're the world's worst furnace."

I demanded to sleep alone, but Saint refused to comply. Admittedly, I slept better than I have in months. Maybe in my whole life. But I'll be damned if I let him know that. I still can't fully trust him with my eyes open, let alone closed for eight hours. He's already tied me up once while I was in bed.

"Are you ready for day one of your writing retreat?" he asks.

A spark of excitement ignites in my chest. Maybe I should keep fighting him. Demand he take me back home. I know he has no intentions of letting me return after this month-long writing retreat. He wants me to live with him. To stay here forever.

But I can't bring myself to want to return. Not yet.

"I am." I straighten and his thumb grazes the side of my mouth, swiping away a streak of syrup. He licks the sweet liquid from his skin, devious tongue glinting as it slips past his lips, and I swallow the lump in my throat.

The only reason everything this man does is attractive is because he's made me come harder than I ever have in my life. Three times. My brain is temporarily discombobulated by sex hormones. That's all.

Saint holds out his hand to me like I'm royalty. His delicious ink-and-paper scent envelops me as I slide my palm into his, and he threads our fingers together to lead me from the room.

Last night, as his car climbed the long drive up to his manor, it dawned on me how truly secluded we are up here. There are no other houses for miles.

We descend the gently curved staircase and my bare feet slap against the pristine flooring. All of the walls are black or deep shades of gray, most of the decor onyx and gold. Chandeliers droop from the towering ceilings and tiny gargoyles and candelabra adorn the staircase.

"Are you a witch?"

He winks at me. "In the sense that I have a magic touch and a broomstick you can ride whenever you wish."

I roll my eyes, even as his words make desire pool low in my belly. The dining room table is mahogany and massive, capable of seating twelve. "Do you often entertain guests?"

"Not if I can help it."

I grin. Neither would I.

"This is the sunroom." He drops my hand to pull apart two sliding glass doors. We step down into another room with floor-to-ceiling windows on every exterior wall and a door that leads to the tranquil backyard. "The windows are tinted so you can see out, but no one can see in."

"Like there's anyone around to spy on us." Maybe I should be terrified about being so secluded with my stalker—now kidnapper—but I'm not. I'm savoring the peace away from all the distractions of normal life.

In the corner, a waterfall fountain gently flows, giving the room a tranquil effect. In the middle of the room, two chairs are set up with laptops on the coffee table in front of them. On the trays beside the chairs are two steaming cups of coffee and two plates lined with cheese and crackers. My favorite writing snack.

"What do you think, muse?" he purrs. "Will this suffice?"

Suffice. This is the kindest gesture anyone has ever made for me. Still, a part of me can't admit that he's winning this game. "Most likely."

Saint guides me by the hand to my chair and sits beside me

in his, where we stay for the next several hours, sipping from our coffees, munching on our snacks, and typing on keyboards. Every once in a while, his hand lands on another part of my body—my shoulder, my neck, my arm, my leg, my knee. Every time his touch grazes my skin, I stare at my computer screen and fail to type another word for the next ten minutes, too distracted thinking about all of the other places I want him touching me.

"I'm glad you're here, muse." His warm voice breaks the silence, dark eyes so full of adoration and joy, the unfamiliar lump returns to my throat.

Saint wasn't lying—everything he's done has been for me, to make me happy. Breaking into my house, tying me up, and kidnapping me to bring me to his estate for winter break was probably the best thing he could've done.

No one has ever done something so kind and thoughtful for me. No one has ever taken my writing seriously enough to care. Maybe only another writer could be capable of a gesture like this.

Or maybe only Saint de Haas.

CHAPTER TWO
SAINT

With my muse by my side in the library, I revised the first third of my manuscript today. She managed to crack five thousand words in her own project, which made me grin in absolute delight. She refused to let me read a single word of it, and I'm dying to know what story had her so enraptured. If I inspire her just as much as she inspires me.

Her brows are adorably furrowed in concentration as she researches literary agencies. Half of the time I've spent working on my manuscript, she's spent scrutinizing agents and compiling a list for me to query.

She's tenacious in her quest to find me the best possible representation.

"You should become a literary agent," I tell her.

If Briar was an agent, she could represent me. No one would fight as doggedly for me as she would. She has just the right amount of assertiveness and passion to be the perfect advocate for so many writers. She'd certainly outperform the Derriks of the literary world.

Her eyes don't move from the screen. "I already have a job."

"But this one you could do in your pajamas, and you'd get to work with your favorite author." I wink at her.

"I'm sure it takes years to become an agent. You need someone who can represent you now."

"Then you better get started." I snap my laptop shut. "I'm going to run you that bath you've been fantasizing about."

She lights up before schooling her features and returning her focus to her screen. She's still fighting her affection for me, but I have plenty of time to open her eyes to her true feelings.

When I call her up, she takes in a breath at the bath I've drawn for her. Black petals float across the surface, vanilla-scented candles lit in each corner, and a small flame dances in the fireplace at the edge of the tub. The massive window gives her a clear view of the dark forest beneath us.

"The view is even more stunning during the day," I promise.

She's grinning and manages a single nod. "Thank you." The words are curt, gratitude unfamiliar on her lips, especially when directed toward me. But I'll take it.

"Whatever I can give, you shall receive. You'll get your massage after."

Her magnetizing blue eyes light up. "What if I want my massage now? In the tub."

My black heart stutters. Briar has never initiated the intimacy between us before.

She's finally opening up to me.

I gesture to the tub. "Consider your wish granted."

By the time I shut the door, she's stripping off her clothes and climbing into the water. I catch a glimpse of her bare, round ass before she dips beneath the surface. I'll be taking my time massaging her tight glutes tonight. I'm sure her ass and back are sore from sitting all day. Soon, I'll have her sore in another way.

Briar keeps her gaze trained on me as I slowly strip in front of her, lazily unfastening every button on my shirt before reaching for the buckle on my belt.

"Let me help," she says sweetly, hands reaching for the buckle and deftly unfastening it. She tugs my pants and boxers down, clearing her throat when she unsheathes my erection.

I slide into the tub behind her, and she freezes like she's bracing herself for whatever I'm about to do to her.

When I lather my hands with lavender soap and sink my thumbs into the tight knots at her shoulders, her muscles relax and she sighs, leaning back into my touch.

I take my time, rubbing every inch of her soft, supple body. From her shoulders, down her arms, giving extra attention to her wrists, hands, and fingers. I repeat the motion down her other arm. She's so limp in my hands now, she can barely keep herself upright.

My fingers explore her back, massaging away every knot before I kiss down each notch of her spine. She releases a small, satisfied sigh. I lather up my hands again before tilting her back against me and reaching around to massage her breasts.

Her breath catches. "You must be a witch because these hands are magical."

I chuckle. "You must be a goddess because these tits were made to be worshipped."

"That's right. I am," she simpers.

After I gently massage her breasts and stomach, her body tightens again as she anticipates my hands between her legs. Instead, I pour water over her head and rub shampoo into her hair.

She groans. "Few things are better than a scalp massage."

"What things are better?" I tease.

"A tongue massage."

My cock twitches at the memory of my tongue between her legs. I'll give her that massage soon enough.

After rinsing the shampoo from her hair, I bend her knees up to knead at the tight muscles in her legs. She groans at the strain when I wash her foot but bites back her complaint once my fingers dig into the soles. Every inch of her is so soft, so pliable, surrendering to even my lightest touch.

When I nudge her knees back down into the water, my muse

groans. "This is the best massage I've ever had, and you haven't even grazed my pussy."

"We need to save the best for last, don't we?"

My hand slips down into the water, sliding across her parted thighs until finally dipping between her legs. One hand massages her inner thigh while the other rubs gently at her clit, already swollen and ready for me. Her breath hitches and she grips my legs to anchor herself.

I suck on the freshly cleaned skin on her neck as she moans for me. "Correction," she pants. "*This* is the best massage I've ever gotten."

The hand on her inner thigh slips down, and I slide a finger inside her, massaging her pussy. She's so tight and tense, her walls grip my finger in a chokehold. She whimpers.

"Are you going to come like this, muse?" I murmur in her ear.

"I could," she admits, breathless. "But I want to come on your cock."

There she is. My muse. Inviting me into her body. Soon, she'll invite me into her heart.

"Do you trust me? It's very important that you trust me, Briar."

In order to do to her what I have planned, to earn her love, I need her trust.

She takes a moment to consider. The silence falling between us makes my spine go rigid until she utters, "I'm trying."

My eyes fall briefly shut at the small victory. We're making progress. Soon, she'll trust me completely. With her heart, body, and soul.

"Then get on your hands and knees."

Briar does as she's told, water sloshing as she tips forward, hands sinking beneath the water as her back and ass rise out. She is glistening and eager for me, a magnificent sight I long to devour.

I caress her ass in my hands. So smooth and slick, begging to be taken. "What's our safe word, muse?"

"We shouldn't need a safe word," she snipes.

My fingers reach up to pinch and twist her nipple. She yelps. "If we don't need a safe word, you're not ready for what I'm going to do to you."

"Grave."

"Grave?"

Her eyes blaze as she glares at me over her shoulder. "As in, that's the next place you'll find yourself if you keep doing that to me."

My grin stretches from ear to ear. "Perfect."

With one hand, I find her clit, and with the other, I nudge my cock at her entrance. Her muscles tighten as she prepares herself for the intrusion, and I slide slowly in, the tight walls of her pussy nearly impossible to penetrate.

She cries out, back arching and head swinging up. "Fuck! Please tell me the whole thing is in."

I laugh. God, she makes me laugh like no one else. "Not even close, muse. You have several more inches to take."

She groans, attempting to push back into me and take more of my cock until she yelps and jerks forward, nearly every inch sliding out of her.

I gather her hair in my hand, continuing to play with her clit to relax her for me. "Let your pussy acclimate to my cock. We've got all night, muse."

A whimper from low in her throat is music to my ears. "The writing retreat was just a front, wasn't it?" she pants. "This is the real reason you brought me here. To fuck me in every room of your giant manor."

I ease my cock back in slowly, pulling her hair as I do and craning her neck up. "I brought you here to write." I tug on her hair, making her yelp. "This is just a bonus."

Her moan sends desire down to my toes. "The writing is the bonus to me."

My black heart swells. Briar has fallen for this part of me—the part that can make her come so hard, she screams my name and loses all sense of self. Now I just need her to fall in love with my soul, no matter how dark and fractured it may be.

"Remember our safe word, muse?" I drive my cock inside her, spearing her pussy as her walls throb around me. She feels so fucking good.

She cries out at the delicious combination of pleasure and pain. "Yes."

I tighten my grip on her wet hair. "Good. You may need it."

With that, I shove her head underwater, water splashing as I slam into her so hard, her ass bounces against me with an echoing slap and her submerged head nearly hits the edge of the tub.

I yank her hair up to let her breathe as I thrust inside her twice more, her ass smacking back against my pelvis and the water sloshing violently around us.

She gasps for air. "What the *fuck*—"

I push her head down again, grinding my fingers hard against her clit while I slam into her sweet pussy, tighter than she's ever been at the tension from not being able to breathe while she gets fucked.

My thrusts pick up speed as she starts to squirm beneath my hand, still keeping her submerged in the water. Our bodies are slippery, the echoes of our wet skin smacking together obscene. Pleasure makes the hairs on the back of my neck stand up. I could come inside her any second.

Finally, I let her back up, and she gulps down air again. I wait for our safe word to sputter from her lips, but it doesn't. She braces her hands on both sides of the tub, trying to keep me from pushing her back down while she fills her lungs with air. "This is so fucked!"

"And yet you already know this is going to be the most intense orgasm of your life, don't you?"

"Fuck you!" she spits. When I drive my cock into her harder, she gasps. "Agh! *Fuck!*"

"Let go of the tub, muse," I instruct.

"No, you're going to drown me."

"I won't let you drown. You said you trusted me. Either you trust me or you don't."

I'm uncertain what she's going to choose—to keep fighting me, keep her palms braced on the tub, or to let her hands fall back in the water and put her trust in me.

Slowly, her white knuckles slacken, and her hands inch down the edges of the tub to rest in the water below her.

"That's it, muse," I murmur. "I'll let you come now."

I shove her head back underwater, slamming my cock into her as hard as I can on the slippery surface. My frantic fingers on her sensitive clit make it throb until her pussy is clenching and pulsing around my cock, the orgasm finally sweeping over her.

She writhes beneath me, screaming underwater, and the sight and sound of her unraveling is my own undoing. My cock jumps inside her pussy, ropes of cum shooting out before I even feel my balls tighten.

Pleasure coils around my spine and sings through my veins, eyes aching to fall shut, but I can't let her out of my sight. Not when my cock has her in the throes of ecstasy.

With the final spurt of my cum inside her, I groan and allow her to resurface, water pouring off her glistening skin and sopping hair.

She collapses at the edge of the tub, heaving as she comes down from her orgasm and sucks air into her oxygen-starved lungs. "Next time," she pants. "I'm going to drown you in my pussy."

I smirk. "And I eagerly anticipate it."

When the month is over, my muse won't fight to leave. She'll be begging to stay.

CHAPTER THREE

BRIAR

I<small>N</small> S<small>AINT'S</small> <small>BED,</small> <small>AWAY</small> <small>FROM</small> <small>HIS</small> <small>PRYING</small> <small>EYES,</small> I <small>RESEARCH</small> how to become a literary agent.

Before I settled on a more practical career path, I wanted to work in book publishing. Then I realized New York is crazy expensive and everyone in publishing is criminally overworked and underpaid. Still, part of me can't help entertaining the idea of interning twenty hours a week at a literary agency. I have no clue how I would balance an internship with my day job, but I haven't been able to get the possibility out of my head since Saint suggested it. I would be a kick-ass agent, and I'd get to work with authors and books all day. I'd attend exclusive publishing events with other agents, editors, and authors. I'd get to travel to conventions and festivals and attend book signings. The right agency might even let me work fully remote in my pajamas.

If I can become an agent and make the right connections, I wouldn't settle for anything less than the best for S.T. Nicholson's books. After all the shit Saint has been through in his life, he at least deserves a successful career he's worked hard for. Not to mention I want to fill up my S.T. Nicholson shelf with signed books.

My phone rings with a call from Trevor. I texted everyone letting them know I'd be off the grid during winter break on a solo writing retreat, so I'm not sure why he's calling.

Mom was over the moon, texting in all caps with three exclamation points at the end of every sentence to let me know she's happy I'm focusing on my passion again. Mack said she was insulted I didn't invite her and that she better be invited on the next writing retreat.

> And what are you going to do on a writing retreat?

> What all the great writers do, obviously. Drink.

Since then, they've all been giving me space to concentrate and fully immerse myself in my writing. Until now.

When Trevor calls again, I sigh and swipe my thumb across the screen. Up until a few months ago, we were only work friends, but since I involved him in helping me prove Saint's criminal activity, he's almost like a real friend now. "Trevor, listen, I can't talk. I'm on my writing retreat, remember? It's supposed to be this zen, distraction-free time to fully immerse myself in my book."

Not that Saint has been particularly helpful with the distraction-free part. Not when his hands drift around my body of their own accord while I'm writing. Not when he whispers seductive words in my ear when I'm mid-sentence. Certainly not when he was shoving my head underwater while he fucked me.

I still can't believe he did. I can't believe I *let* him. Or that I loved it so much. Who would've thought near-drowning would be the next kink I unlocked.

"Shit, sorry. I won't keep you," Trevor says quickly. "I just wanted to make sure you're okay."

Great. Now I'm the jackass. "Yeah, I'm fine. I've had my phone off."

"Okay, good. I just wanted to make sure." His voice brightens. "I'm still looking into your stalker, so don't worry. We'll get this guy locked up. Sorry it's taking so long. He's sneakier than I thought he'd be."

Trevor has no idea.

"Actually, you don't have to keep looking anymore. I don't want to press charges."

Stunned silence as Trevor lets my words sink in. I bite my lip, second-guessing if maybe I shouldn't have admitted that out loud. What possible sane explanation could I give him to justify why I no longer want to prove Saint has been stalking me and killing the men around me?

The next words out of Trevor's mouth are hesitant. "Briar, be honest with me, okay? Are you . . . falling in love with your stalker?"

"I'm not in love with him." The words tumble out of my mouth reflexively, except . . . I'm not totally sure they're true anymore.

Maybe I'm not in love with him yet, but I can't deny anymore that I am falling.

Saint de Haas has done the impossible—not only has he made me admit to myself that I'm falling in love, but he's made me start falling for my stalker. For a serial killer.

"Good. I've profiled guys like him. They're master manipulators. But I know you're smart enough not to fall for it."

I'm close to telling him someone's intelligence has nothing to do with how well they can be manipulated, but I bite my tongue. "Yeah, don't worry about me."

He laughs. "You're my friend, Briar. I'll always worry about you. Anyway, I'll let you get back to your writing retreat. See you next semester."

"See you."

When I hang up, Saint raps on the door and pokes his head in the room with a feline smile. I jump, praying he didn't overhear that conversation. "I love seeing you in my clothes."

14

"If you had let me pack a bag before kidnapping me from my house, I could've brought my own."

When Saint said he packed our bags for us, I stupidly thought he stole clothes from my dresser or at the very least bought women's clothes for me. Instead, article after article of clothing I pulled from the bag was full of loose, oversized men's attire, all of it coated in his ink-and-paper scent.

"I need my muse to read my latest chapter." He holds out his hand to me and leads the way downstairs.

His laptop rests on the kitchen island, and he hovers nearby while I read the scene on the screen. It's so clearly fanfiction of us, I snort. In the scene, "Belle" and "Simon" have just committed murder, and they're racing from the crime scene until they find a dark alley, where Simon picks her up, holds her against the wall, and fucks her, both of them still covered in blood and wearing their masks.

His imagination is absolutely sick and depraved, and my lips should definitely not be curling up into a smile.

"It's really too bad I don't have a mask," I purr. "Maybe we can act this scene out sometime. For research purposes, of course. To verify the realism of the angles and physics."

"In the meantime . . ." Saint strides for the light switch, plummeting us into darkness. When his hands land on my hips, he's wearing his mask. ". . . Maybe we can act out one of your favorite scenes."

My breath catches. I hope to god he's talking about the first spicy scene in his debut novel, where the masked serial killer fucks the heroine on her kitchen table.

Saint lifts me by the back of my thighs and I wrap my legs around him. He plants my ass on the massive mahogany dining table. "Ah. So this is why you bought this table."

"Exactly, muse," he growls.

He yanks the shirt over my head first, my eyes still adjusting to the darkness and my heart already racing in anticipation.

"Are we going to be acting out every sex scene you've ever written?" I ask. "Because you've written a lot of them."

I can't see his mouth beneath his mask, but I know he's smirking. "Sounds like we'll be here for a while then."

His expert fingers travel to the waistband of the boxers around my middle and yank them down my legs.

"I believe he feasted on the heroine for an hour. If I'm not mistaken."

His chuckle echoes in his mask. "Yes, he didn't quite have the endurance of his author."

"You're saying you could lick my pussy for over an hour?" I challenge.

"I'm saying I will lick you until my tongue falls off if that's what you desire."

My god, this man. "If your tongue falls off, what use would I have for you?"

He yanks me to the edge of the table, my bare ass squeaking across the surface. "My fingers and cock could still make you scream."

I trace the painted flames on his mask that dance along his cheek, then glide my fingers across the inhuman white smile that both sends a shiver down my spine and makes my pussy clench.

To prove his point, he doesn't lift his mask up to pleasure me with his mouth. Instead, his hands wrench my thighs apart, and his fingers find my clit, eliciting a moan from my lips. "You'll never question what use you have for me again, muse."

I whimper as he tears off my bra, ripping through the flimsy fabric and rendering it useless.

I grind my teeth. "That's the only bra I had because someone wouldn't let me pack more."

"The fewer the clothes, the better. I fully intend on forcing you to walk around our home naked."

Our home. Like I already live here with him. Saint de Haas is the most presumptuous, delusional, alluring man I've ever met. "And what if I get cold?"

"What have I told you, muse?" he growls and unsheathes his cock, not bothering to remove any of his clothes. Even though I ache to see every inch of him just as his eyes feast on me, there's something arousing about him remaining fully covered while he nudges his tip at my entrance. "I will give you everything you need."

Without another word, he buries his cock inside me, warming me from the inside out.

I scream at the unexpected intrusion, the stretch around his thick length painful. "Agh! Fuck!"

Saint rubs at my sensitive nub, making my sore pussy throb, but the pleasure makes his cock slide in and out of my tight walls with greater ease.

My ass squeaks against the table and my tits bounce with every hard thrust. He slaps one, making me yelp as my skin reddens. I'm not sure what I've unleashed to make him so rough with me, but I fucking love it.

In my peripheral vision, I catch a flash of movement. Saint's thumb on my clit and his cock in my pussy drive pleasure up all the way to the tip of my scalp, and the ecstasy nearly blinds me to what's lingering in the darkness outside the window.

Who.

A face hidden in the shadows of the night. But their hand rests against the glass.

My heart stops.

"Someone's outside the window!"

Saint shoves his mask up and pinches my cheeks between his thumb and forefinger, forcing my eyes to lock on his blazing, coal-black gaze as he continues fucking me. "There is no one else in existence when I'm inside you."

He's crazy. We need to stop. "But what if—"

"I don't give a fuck if the entire nation is standing outside that window watching us," he growls. "They don't exist. Nothing else exists right now except you and me. You're my whole world now, muse, and I'm yours."

CHAPTER FOUR

SAINT

EVERY TIME BRIAR'S ATTENTION STARTS TO DRIFT TO THE window while I slam my cock inside her, I wrap a hand around her throat and squeeze. "Eyes on me, muse."

No one is outside this manor. I own the whole fucking mountain, and it's the middle of winter in Maine. No one is going for a hike up here.

Or perhaps she really did see what she thinks—a lost hiker searching for refuge. And now I suppose they're getting a show.

I don't give a fuck. They can watch my glistening cock drive inside her tight pussy over and over. They can listen to her moans and wails as she takes every hard inch, clenching and spasming each time I hit that sweet spot deep inside her. They can jerk off to us fucking on the dining room table for all I care. As long as she remembers that nothing outside this room matters when I'm inside her. The house could be burning down around us and I wouldn't stop fucking her until she came on my cock.

I overheard her on the phone. Heard her say she's not in love with me. Spitting out the words like the idea of loving me repulses her. But I know her well enough by now to understand she's in denial. If she wasn't falling in love with me, she wouldn't be here. She wouldn't have let me fuck her after I taped her wrists and ankles together, she wouldn't have let me whisk her away to my secluded manor, and she wouldn't be on this table with her legs spread wide, allowing my dick to split her pussy in two.

But I'm still proving myself to her. Still proving my worth. That she will fall in love with me someday. That she will be mine forever.

"Agh! Saint!" she moans, nails biting into my triceps.

I keep my mask off, needing her to see how my eyes bore into her all the way to her soul. How my gaze doesn't ever drift from her. From her writhing, glorious, naked body in front of me. To the tits that bounce wildly with every hard, punishing thrust. To the bottom lip, swollen and red from where she bites it in between moans. To the lust-filled blue eyes that roll and flutter shut before springing open through the waves of pleasure.

Her body is the instrument that only I can play.

When her pussy starts to clench on my cock, my name about to leave her lips on a cry, I pump fast into her, chasing both of our orgasms.

"Saint!" she wails.

She screams out for me, not for a god. She may be my muse, but I am her deity.

I keep thrusting inside her as her pussy pulses around me and hot cum shoots from my cock, making my eyes roll. My thrusts are shallow now, but just as hard, her cries of ecstasy the soundtrack to my greatest pleasure.

Sweat coats the back of my neck, heart pounding against my ribcage. *Fuck.* Nothing is sweeter than her.

We pant against each other, coming down from the pinnacle of ecstasy. As soon as I slide out of her and release my hold on her neck, she gasps, legs collapsing to the table and fingers brushing her throat. "I swear to god if you left fingerprints on my neck, they better be gone before I go back home."

At some point, I'll inform her I have no intention of

returning her, but it's too soon to broach the subject. Not until she's falling to her knees, begging to never be parted from me.

She tugs her clothes back in place before diverting her gaze to the same window that distracted her earlier. "Do you have a Peeping Tom neighbor or something?"

"I don't have neighbors. No one else lives on my mountain."

She snorts. "What do you mean *your* mountain?"

"I mean, I own this mountain."

"You *own* a mountain?"

"Yes, and once you marry me, so will you."

She scoffs. "I've already told you marriage is never happening. Not with you or anybody."

"Not with anybody," I confirm. "But undoubtedly with me."

Briar rolls her eyes, rubbing away the goosebumps springing up on her arms as she stares out the window. "Can we look around, at least? Scope out the place to make sure no one's out there?"

"There is a private cemetery nearby. Perhaps you saw a ghost." My taunt elicits an adorable scowl. "Or I suppose it could've been the groundskeeper. He's usually not up here this time of year, let alone this time of night, but I always suspected he held certain . . . disturbing proclivities. I may or may not have based my necrophiliac protagonist on him."

Thirty seconds after shaking the man's hand, various scenarios were darting through my mind in which he snuck around the cemetery at night to defile corpses. I wouldn't doubt he possesses a voyeurism kink as well.

Briar's nose scrunches. "So maybe he wants to kill us and fuck our dead bodies? We definitely need to make sure we're alone then. I won't be able to sleep with a necrophiliac gravedigger running around."

"I can secure the property while you stay inside where it's safe."

"No," she says quickly. "I'm staying with you. Haven't you

ever seen a horror movie? The second you split up, that's when you both die. Or at least, that's when the pretty girl dies."

My muse doesn't want to part from me. A few months ago, I was the person she trusted the least. The person she was most afraid of. Now, she's trusting me to keep her safe. "Very well then. Stay by my side and don't leave my sight."

She rolls her eyes at my order and grumbles, "I'm the one who just said we shouldn't split up."

Our footsteps echo across the dark hardwood floor. By the front doors, I grab a pistol from the secret compartment behind an innocuous shelf.

"Do you have a secret gun collection stashed around your house?" Briar hisses.

"Only a gun for each of my enemies." I flash her a wicked grin.

"Insane," she mumbles.

I grab the loaded magazines, dropping two into my pocket and shoving one into the grip, racking the pistol with a metallic *thunk*. Hot and loaded.

We bundle up before heading out the door, and I shine the flashlight on my gun around the property as we slowly and silently make our way around the perimeter. Snow flurries fall gently in the night, flakes catching in Briar's dark hair as the icy fingers of winter caress our exposed skin.

If there were any footprints marking someone's path around my property, they're gone now.

Briar lets out a small gasp. "There!"

"Where?" I hiss, unable to see where she's pointing in the dark, and I'm sure as hell not aiming my fucking gun at her.

"To the left!"

I send the beam of light to where she directs. But there's nothing around us other than snow and trees. Not even deer tracks mar the snow's undisturbed surface.

"Shit," she murmurs. "Just a tree."

"Let's check the cemetery."

"Great. I love exploring creepy graveyards at night," she grumbles, but she sticks by my side as we make the trek across the hard, compact snow.

Each of our footsteps crunches in the silence until we reach the wrought iron gate and open it with an ominous creak.

"Horror films aren't this terrifying," Briar whispers as my flashlight sweeps over the row of headstones dusted with snow.

We search for our voyeur, but it quickly becomes clear that no one else is out here. The only movement comes from the falling white flakes. We're surrounded by nothing but forest and the hidden wildlife hunkered down for the night. Even the stars and moonlight are concealed by clouds. A world all to ourselves.

"Why are there only seven headstones?" Briar asks.

"It's a private cemetery owned by the family who once owned the manor. The grandson didn't have any children. That was the end of the bloodline."

"You don't worry about mourners showing up?"

I shake my head. "Everyone they knew is dead."

She hugs her arms to her chest, and the creative wheels turn in her head as she contemplates how she can write a story about the departed, wealthy family who once owned the private cemetery on the mountain. "It's so peaceful here."

Snowflakes falling from the sky, far from the disturbance of civilization, offer a unique tranquility. "That's why I chose this mountain for my residence. A writer's mind craves peace, lest he not hear the whisper of words in his head."

"The perfect place for a writing retreat."

"The perfect place for us."

She swallows at my words before rubbing her arms. Not yet convinced I can turn her fantasy—this serene life of seclusion she longs for—into reality. "I think we've established that we're alone up here. Let's head back."

I lead the way to Nicholson Manor, allowing Briar to enter first before I cast one final sweep over the front yard, illuminated by my flashlight and the light pouring from the windows. Nothing.

Inside, I drop the magazine from the pistol and remove the loaded round from the chamber before returning the pistol to its secret compartment.

"Do you think whoever was out there could be a private investigator?" Briar chews her lip.

I quirk a brow. "Why would a PI be up here?"

"I'm pretty sure some blonde woman in a black BMW has been tailing me. She followed me to work one morning, and then I saw her again on campus."

My fists clench. "Why am I just now hearing about this?"

"Because I haven't seen her in a while." My muse shrugs. "I thought the police were just keeping an eye on me."

I close the distance between us, towering over her as I jerk her chin up. "From now on, you don't keep secrets from me."

She rolls her eyes. "It wasn't a secret—I just didn't think to tell you."

"No more secrets."

Briar jerks out of my grasp. "Fine. Whatever. I'm going to bed."

In the bedroom, she strips down, her perfect breasts bouncing when she pulls the shirt over her head. I'll never again know a day when I can keep my hands off her.

"I'm exhausted." Her eyes narrow as she slips under the duvet. "And sore. So we're just sleeping."

I slide in behind her, wrapping an arm around her to fondle one of those perfect tits. She groans softly. Her half-naked body molds perfectly against mine.

I disappear under the blanket. "My tongue won't make you sore."

CHAPTER FIVE
BRIAR

Saint insists I stay behind to get some writing done while he runs into town to grab food. The gesture is thoughtful, but I can't shake off the image of someone watching us fuck through his window. I've been paranoid for days. Nothing more than a fear response after years of conditioning from watching entirely too many true crime documentaries and horror movies, but now that I'm alone in Saint's giant—admittedly spooky—manor, I can't concentrate on writing.

I reach for my phone. Only ten percent battery remaining, but I call Mom anyway.

"Briar! How are you, sweetheart?" Her voice instantly soothes me, like I'm at home and not completely and utterly alone in a manor pulled straight from an S.T. Nicholson Gothic horror novel.

"Hey, Mom. I just wanted to check in."

"How's your writing coming along?"

"Great," I admit. I haven't written so much or so quickly in years. Not even during my MFA program. I've been too busy with work to throw myself into my writing like this since summer breaks from school. I forgot how much I loved writing, convincing myself somewhere along the line that my dream job was becoming a professor to teach other people how to write because that career at least offered financial stability and paid days off.

But what this retreat has taught me is that my true passion lies in books. Devouring them and creating them. While I do still enjoy teaching and I love seeing the progress my students make, nothing else fills me with this level of passion.

Except maybe Saint de Haas. The reason I'm here in the first place. The reason I'm having this self-revelation.

Not that I will ever, ever admit that to him.

"I'm so glad, sweetheart," Mom enthuses. "You needed to take some time for yourself. That Saint certainly seems to know what's best for you."

Panic pricks up my neck. "What does this have to do with Saint?" I told her I came on this writing retreat alone.

"Saint let me know he suggested the retreat. He wanted to make sure I knew you were staying somewhere safe. These gifts he's been sending me are so thoughtful!"

"What gifts?"

"Oh, they're so sweet! You know those chocolate chip blossoms we always make for your birthday? He sent me a batch of those. Then he sent me those dark chocolates and a bouquet of yellow carnations that you get me every year for Mother's Day. And he sent me this *beautiful* scarf! You know how I love scarves. I'll have to send you a picture."

"No, Mom—"

But she's already removed the phone from her ear, fumbling with the various buttons and options on her screen to figure out how to take a photo and send it to me. When she bought her phone, I dedicated at least three hours to teaching her how to use it before giving up.

I check the battery percentage on mine. Five percent. "Mom, my phone's about to die—"

"There! I sent it," she shouts, victorious.

She actually managed to take a photo—albeit, a blurry one

—of a white scarf dangling around the collar of her coat. It's not a scarf I would wear, but it's exactly to her taste.

Saint sent her all these gifts to remind her of me in my absence. Small, thoughtful gifts to make my mother happy. And he never breathed a word about them to me.

No matter how many times I try to convince myself that I should hate this man, that I should be repulsed by his obsessive and possessive behaviors, repulsed by the unhinged violence he can unleash on a whim, he makes it impossible.

In all their years of marriage, my father never once got my mother a single gift outside of the obligatory birthdays and holidays, seldom celebrating the occasion with more than a bland card that contained nothing personal written on the inside other than his name.

Saint has set a standard that no other man can possibly reach. A standard I never would've thought possible until I met him.

"Does this mean you and Saint are finally a couple?" my mother asks. I don't have to see her to know she's grinning with her fingers crossed.

"We're not a couple," I blurt. "But . . . I don't know. Maybe . . . we could be. Someday."

The words are more difficult to extract from my mouth than a tooth. Saint and I are certainly acting like a couple on this retreat. Spending every day together, writing side-by-side, and fucking morning, noon, and night. As much as I hate to admit it to myself, I'm falling for him.

And it's terrifying. Not because he's a stalker or a serial killer, but because I know if I let down the walls guarding my heart, he could take it.

"You have no idea how happy that makes me, honey. Honestly, Saint seems to treat you better than your father ever treated me, even in our good days."

Their good days. It's weird to think that my mother and father ever had good days. What if these are simply my and Saint's good days? Maybe this is nothing more than a honeymoon phase. Him on his best behavior, doing everything he can to woo me, and once I let him in, once I'm in too deep, he'll show his true colors. His feelings for me will diminish and he'll no longer shower me with lavish gifts and gestures because he's not chasing me anymore. He'll get bored of me and find another woman to chase. Just like my father always did. He didn't chase women—he chased a prize. And once he got his hands on it, he left it on his trophy shelf with all the others to collect dust, forgotten.

I won't be some forgotten, neglected trophy.

"Did my father RSVP to the wedding?"

Mom sighs. "Yes, Julia let me know he'd be there. But don't worry about me. I'll have no problem avoiding your father with two hundred guests in attendance."

My phone's battery drops to one percent.

"Speaking of your father, I was going to ask you—"

"Mom, I have to go. My phone's really about to die."

"Okay, sweetheart, I love you. Have a great time on the rest of your writing retreat. Tell Saint I say hi!"

"I love you too," I say quickly before hanging up.

I lunge for my phone charger, but the light above my head flickers out. When I plug my phone in, it doesn't charge.

Shit. The power's out. I try to turn on the flashlight on my phone, but it dies.

Of fucking course. I have no clue where the breaker is in this giant house, and now I can't call Saint to tell him to get his ass home to turn the power back on.

I don't even know where he keeps any of his emergency supplies. But I do know there are still candles around the bathtub and hopefully a lighter.

I fumble my way to the bathroom, keeping my hand glued to the wall to guide my path. In the bathroom, I manage to grasp a lighter near the sink and a half-burnt candle on the tub.

The flickering wick doesn't offer much light, but it's better than nothing.

A thud from downstairs makes my spine stiffen. "Saint?"

The small flame dances near my cupped hand and the hairs on the back of my neck rise in the ensuing silence. Saint's voice doesn't come.

Maybe something fell. Maybe it was snow falling off a branch outside or a rodent in the walls. Better yet, maybe the sound was nothing more than my imagination.

Who am I kidding? It's a fucking murderer who's here to kill me now that I'm alone.

And I just let them know exactly where to find me.

My heart thuds, and I race back to the bedroom to grab the gun Saint keeps in his bedside drawer. Not that I have any fucking clue how to use it. How do I even load the thing?

When I yank the drawer open, my heart stops.

The gun is gone. *Shit.* Saint must've taken it with him.

Fuck. *Fuck, fuck, fuck.*

I don't know where he keeps any of his other secret weapons up here. For all I know, he was joking about owning a gun for each of his enemies and there's only one pistol left in this house —the one beside the front doors.

The intruder is between me and my only hope for survival.

In the darkness, footsteps creep slowly up the winding staircase. I stop breathing, sliding the drawer silently shut. What the hell do I do? I don't have a weapon to fight off whoever's in the house with me, and they sure as hell didn't break into Nicholson Manor unarmed.

I'm outmatched. In a mansion I'm completely unfamiliar with. But if this is a stranger, they've likely never been in Nicholson Manor at all. At least I have a slight edge there, especially in the dark.

I set the flickering candle down on the bedside table and sneak across the wide hall to Saint's office, the footsteps of the intruder reaching the top of the staircase.

Sucking in a deep, silent breath and holding it, I listen intently as the intruder dares to shuffle down the hallway. My nails curl into fists as I flatten my back against the wall beside the door.

The floorboards creak under the intruder's weight, growing slightly fainter as they follow my candle into Saint's bedroom. I can't tell if the footsteps belong to a man or a woman.

I dare a peek around the open doorway, hoping I'll find Saint's towering frame and laugh in relief.

But the intruder has already extinguished the burning flame on the candle. Plunging the room into darkness and them into the shadows.

I don't give the intruder time to turn and find me watching them in the dark. I break into a sprint, lungs burning as I run faster and harder than I ever have in my life.

Footsteps thunder behind me, tearing down the staircase and slamming into the railing.

Heart about to burst in my chest, my feet hit the landing, and I hip-check a hard, sharp wooden edge, grimacing at the pain and whatever ceramic decor smashes to the floor behind me.

Seconds later, the intruder's feet crunch over the destroyed ceramic. I slam into the dining room table, yelping as my foot catches on a chair. I go down, palms slamming against the floor and teeth clacking together.

They round into the room, and I'm certain I'm going to get caught until I scramble under the table, leaping to my feet and beelining for the front doors. I fling them shut behind me, a weak attempt to buy some time to hide before they can open the doors and follow my path.

My bare feet scream when I race across the freezing gravel driveway and duck beside the garage. The most obvious place to find me.

But the doors don't open.

What the hell are they doing in there? Did something stop

them? Or are they taking another path? Maybe they opted for a different exit to ambush me.

Or the intruder knows I won't be able to stay out here for long in the cold without shoes or a coat. The freezing winter temperatures a ticking time bomb.

They're waiting me out.

At some point, I'll be forced to choose between freezing to death and being murdered.

CHAPTER SIX
SAINT

My gift for Briar sits on my passenger seat and keeps me grinning the entire way home. Though I'd love to give it to her the second I return, I won't surprise her with it until I'm certain what her reaction will be.

When my headlights hit the garage, Briar is crouching beside the building, staring wide-eyed at Nicholson Manor until her terrified gaze lands on my car.

She leaps up and races toward me, without a coat or shoes. Her toes are going to fall off out here.

I barely throw the car in Park before I'm out the door and rushing for her. "What's wrong?"

"Someone's inside!" she wails, terror changing her voice to something unrecognizable. "They must've broken in, and they chased me! They're still in there!"

Fury ignites inside me. Some monster thinks he can go after my muse. Scare her. Chase her. Hurt her. She's shivering violently in her scraps of clothing and bare feet.

Once I get my hands on him, she and I will both watch the light leave his eyes.

I brace my hands on her shoulders, leaning down so we're

eye-to-eye. "I need you to prepare yourself, Briar. Watching someone die isn't pretty."

Fear flashes in her eyes until she nods, resolute. She's smart. She knows it's either him or her, and she's already made the right decision.

She's glued to my side while I pull my gun from my waistband and head inside, every room encased in shadows.

"I'm pretty sure they cut the power," she whispers.

"Really? I simply assumed you enjoyed dwelling in darkness."

She elbows me in the ribs. "Now isn't the time for your sarcasm."

"There is no bad time for sarcasm."

"A funeral."

"You're kidding. A funeral is the best time for sarcasm."

"Just quit talking and look for the fucking killer stalking through your house."

"Technically, two of us meet that criteria," I whisper.

This situation is all too familiar, and part of me suspects Briar had a nightmare or her paranoia conjured up the groundskeeper or the private investigator she believes she saw watching us fuck through the window. But her terror is real, and I've made too many enemies not to take her words seriously.

I conduct an entire sweep of the house with Briar at my side, sharp talons digging into my forearm. Glad I still have my coat on.

We search in every room, closet, nook, and cranny, Briar making frequent comments like, "I didn't even know this room existed," and "I'm pretty sure I've counted thirty-five rooms. What use could you possibly have for thirty-five rooms?"

But no matter where my flashlight lands, we don't stumble across the mysterious intruder.

We make our way back down to the breaker, and I flip the power on. Other than the hum of the lights and appliances, Nicholson Manor remains silent. We're alone.

Briar whirls on me. "I know what you're thinking—I'm paranoid, I'm delusional, and I need to stop watching so much true crime. But I'm telling you, there was someone in this house. They literally chased me out the door."

"I believe you."

She visibly relaxes at the quick assurance in my tone. "Maybe it's one of those phrogging situations. Somebody moved in while you weren't home and decided to chase me out. The groundskeeper, maybe."

If he really was the one she saw watching us the other night, it's possible he could've decided to take shelter in my empty manor for the winter. I would've happily allowed him to stay in a room if he'd asked. But now that he's chosen to terrorize my muse, he'll be lucky if I allow him to take another breath.

I grab her face in both hands, her skin so soft and delicate and beautiful. In need of my protection. "This is my fault. I should've kept our home more secure. I should've installed a hundred cameras and locks when I knew I was bringing you here. I'm sorry I wasn't here to protect you. That will never happen again. I will never leave your side if it means I can keep you safe."

She scoffs, even though the tiny smile tells me my words bring her comfort. "You can't be by my side twenty-four-seven."

"Watch me."

"Absolutely not. I need my space. If I'm around you constantly, you'll drive me insane. And you're not watching me while I'm on the toilet taking a shit."

"I'll be in the room, but I'll put on headphones and turn my back to give you some privacy."

Her nose scrunches in disgust, and I manage a laugh.

I'm the stupidest man alive for leaving her here alone. For assuming she would be safe, even after what happened to my mother. What nearly happened to me when I was left alone.

I failed to protect my mother, but I won't fail Briar. I can't. I can't lose them both.

I don't care if she doesn't like it. I don't care if she wants her space or wants to push me away. I'm not going anywhere. This is the last time I ever take my eyes off her.

For as long as I'm breathing, I will be the other half of her soul and the shadow at her back.

"Saint?"

"Yes, muse?"

Her eyes are hard, resolute. "I want you to teach me how to kill somebody."

"You wouldn't think a reclusive, anonymous author would have enough enemies to warrant a private shooting range," Briar mumbles. She's adorable in my oversized coat and knit hat.

"Never know when I'll need to brush up on my marksmanship."

We slip on earmuffs and safety goggles. May the universe watch over me as I attempt to survive an afternoon of teaching Briar how to shoot.

"For your first lesson, I'll teach you how to use a pistol." I duck down to murmur in Briar's ear. "Maybe later, I'll show you how to use something bigger."

She smirks, eyes glimmering behind the goggles before she grabs the gun. She waves the pistol around until it's pointing directly at my feet. "Wow, this is surprisingly heavy. So how do I shoot this thing?"

I shove her hands forward, pointing the pistol ahead. *Jesus.* There is no way I'm surviving this. "First rule: never point a gun at anyone or anything you're not willing to shoot. Especially me."

"Even if it's not loaded?"

"*Every* firearm is loaded. Even if you know you dropped the magazine and emptied the chamber. Always treat it like it's loaded so you avoid an accident."

"Okay, so don't point it at you until I'm ready to shoot. Got it." Briar flashes me a naughty smirk.

"Don't make me punish you," I warn, and she stiffens. I step up behind her, brushing her back before caressing her hands as goosebumps spring up along her arms. "Your grip is important for accuracy and safety. Wrap your left hand around the grip like this"—I guide her, balls tightening as my cock rubs against her ass—"and tuck your other hand in to fit beside it. Your right hand should be as high on the grip as possible while staying below the slide. Keep it high to reduce the recoil but below the slide so it doesn't tear through your hand."

"Jesus," my muse hisses. "I thought this thing was supposed to be dangerous to the target, not the shooter."

"This is why you need to learn how to use it properly. The next rule is to keep your finger off the trigger until you're ready to shoot. Rest your finger on the trigger guard so you know you won't fire before you're ready." I guide her finger to the square of metal surrounding the trigger.

My cock grows hard against her ass, and she glances over her shoulder, a smirk pulling at her lips. "Are you going to come in your pants when I finally shoot this thing?"

My hot breath caresses her ear, and she shivers. "If I'm going to come in anything, it's going to be your cunt."

She chokes on air. I will never tire of the effect my words have on her.

"Now drop the gun and I'll teach you how to load a magazine."

"I don't even get to shoot yet?" Briar whines.

"You can't shoot a gun without any bullets." I walk her through how to drop the magazine and load it with ammo, along with where the safety is located and how to flick it on and off. Once the magazine is loaded in her pistol, I lift her arms. "Aim at your target and look down the sight with your dominant eye."

She points the barrel at the nearest target. Before I can walk her through the steps of how to properly prepare herself for the recoil, she pulls the trigger.

The blast makes her yelp, eyes wide behind her goggles. "Holy *fuck!*"

"That's the recoil. Use your shoulders and arms to hold the gun steady. Grip it hard enough to shake and then lighten up until it stops moving."

She does as I instruct, quickly gaining confidence as the pistol remains steady in her hands as she slowly fires off staccato shots. But her aim is terrible.

"Point it at the target, not the trees."

"I'm not pointing it at the trees!"

I'm all too happy to hover behind my muse again, guiding her arms as her round ass pushes back against my cock. Her breathing hitches. "Look down the sight and put the dot on the target."

Once she angles the gun and fires, she finally strikes true, hitting within the red circle. She squeals. "I hit it!"

"Now empty the magazine."

She fires off three more rounds before the trigger clicks with the dull echo of an empty chamber and she pouts.

The sun has descended past the mountain, night swiftly encasing us in darkness. I smile at my muse. "Another round?"

Briar nods eagerly. I didn't expect to enjoy her with a weapon in her hands so much. Her movements are shaky as she loads the magazine with ten rounds of ammo, but she's a quick learner.

I guide her through the proper way to grip the firearm again, even as her eyes roll. "One day of shooting doesn't make you an expert. By the time your training is over, you'll be able to load the magazine and rack the gun with a blindfold on."

"I'm not shooting while blindfolded!"

My turn to roll my eyes. "Of course not. I don't have a death wish."

I release her, and Briar slowly but steadily fires off the ten rounds, landing all but one on the target.

She cheers, dropping the pistol on the table before racing to me and throwing her arms around my neck. My heart soars at her dazzling smile.

Briar rocks up on her toes and pulls my lips down to meet hers in an all-consuming kiss. Every inch of me—from my scalp to my chest to my cock to my toes—ignites. My hands wrap around her, pulling her as close to me as I can. I'll never get enough of the feel of her in my hands, her soft, pouty lips against mine, her pulse hammering against my chest until our heartbeats synchronize and I can no longer distinguish between the two.

She is my salvation.

When she finally pulls away, I'm not ready to let her go. "That was fun," she pants, breathless.

"The gun or my mouth?"

She sneers at the innuendo. "Both."

"I'm impressed, muse." I nod to the shooting range behind her. "You're a quick learner."

"Why are you so surprised I know how to handle a gun?" she purrs, picking up the pistol. "I want to shoot another magazine. The next time someone breaks into any house I'm in, they're not making it out alive."

CHAPTER SEVEN

BRIAR

When I stir awake, I'm greeted by darkness and the scent of old books.

I'm in Saint's library. But something silky and cool shields my eyes.

Fuck.

The intruder.

I jerk against the restraints binding me to the chair, chest heaving rapidly as the air I attempt to suck down comes in shallow, staccato breaths.

I'm naked and tied to a chair.

How did the intruder get me here? How did they take my clothes off, carry me to the library, and tie me down without waking me? They must've drugged me somehow. Rendered me unconscious long enough to get me here.

And if I'm here, they must've done the same to Saint. Or worse.

I open my mouth to scream for Saint when the edge of a sharp blade skims my exposed collarbone.

I freeze, breath hitching as the threat of the knife immobilizes me.

"Shh." A mask distorts the hush, curdles the sound of air

through teeth into something far more sinister. "Quiet. This is a library."

The murmured warning is familiar, relaxing my shoulders taut with tension. But only a little.

"What the hell are you doing, Saint?"

This is what I get for letting my stalker whisk me away to his Gothic manor. I couldn't have been a woman with some shred of sense and stayed the fuck away from him after he broke into my house?

Maybe if I'd thought with my brain instead of my libido, I wouldn't be strapped naked to a chair while my masked stalker trails the edge of a knife over my skin.

"You need to practice how to calm yourself when you're afraid." The knife leaves my collarbone in a fleeting moment of relief. Only to skim along the other, with the sharp edge this time. The blade threatens to slice me open any second. "How to breathe. How to manage your fear. Harness it."

My heart is still thundering from the panicked moments I thought he was the intruder come to kill me. My breaths are still shallow, even as I remind myself that I'm safe. Even naked, tied to a chair, and blindfolded, I'm safer with Saint de Haas than an unknown assailant.

"I'm fucking calm," I spit. "Now untie me."

He chuckles, pulling the knife away. An all-too-familiar, hollow clink of metal follows.

His gun.

"Oh, muse. We're just getting started."

I thrash against the restraints, succeeding only in making my wrists and ankles ache. "At least remove my blindfold."

"A man who wants to kill you won't give you the gift of sight," he bites, pacing around me.

He wants to force me to use my other senses. To track the sound of his steps, to scent our surroundings, to weigh my obstacles and weapons, to taste the fear on my tongue and harness it.

"What did you give me?"

"A small sedative in your dinner. Your full strength should return to you any minute."

The bastard drugged me. Of course a stalker would consider this a twisted form of self-defense training. "Like that will do me any good when you have me tied down."

He trails the barrel of the pistol across my heaving chest. "You're still allowing your fear to control you. Control your fear, Briar. Own your body. Your mind. You are your biggest obstacle."

I squeeze my eyes shut, even though I'm already blindfolded, and force a deep breath through my nose and out of my mouth.

"Good. Now focus on your muscles while you breathe. Relax each group of muscles, concentrate on alleviating the tension. Bend them to your will."

I do as he instructs, forcing my shoulders to relax. The tension slowly slips away as I keep drawing in deep breaths. I try to ignore the barrel of the gun slipping down between my breasts and the handle of the knife returning to caress my cheek as my mind concentrates on relaxing the tight muscles in my back, arms, hands, legs.

"You are doing so well, muse."

His praise makes my heart flutter. Admittedly, so does the gun tracing my inner thighs.

My pulse starts to pick up speed again when the fear mixes with excitement. "Saint—"

"Shh." He presses the flat edge of the knife to my lips, effectively silencing me.

Behind my blindfold, my eyes spring open and my stomach turns, a new layer of sweat pricking up along my neck and back.

His mask brushes my cheek, and I shiver. "Let's see how badly you want me to use my weapons to make you come."

"I don't." The terror builds. I don't know how the fuck he could give me pleasure with a knife or a gun, and I don't want to find out. All I know is that gun is loaded and that knife is very, very sharp.

"I think you do," he purrs. Cool, hard metal brushes against my pussy, and I hiss through my teeth, jerking my hips back in an attempt to get away, but there's no escaping Saint de Haas.

He rubs the barrel of the gun against my pussy again, harder this time, and dips the barrel between my folds. Just enough to drag the proof of my arousal up to my pelvis. "Now I know you do."

Goosebumps race down my arms at his low, seductive drawl. "That doesn't mean anything."

But we both know I'll never convince either of us that everything he does isn't arousing to me. That every brush of his skin against mine doesn't set me on fire in the best possible way.

God, I wish he would remove this fucking blindfold so I could see him. His lithe, toned body towering over me. The muscles in his back and arms rippling with every movement. The mask on his face concealing the dancing, onyx eyes and the delighted smirk. My mouth waters, and I long to break free of the restraints at my wrists just so I can touch him. Admire the lethal power coursing beneath the surface of every inch of taut skin.

"Are you ready to come for me, sinner?"

I swallow. *Sinner.* I'm his muse, his captive, and now, his sinner. "I'm ready for you to take my blindfold off."

"Ah, but that's half the fun. Not knowing when the next touch will come." The knife brushes against my arm, sending tingles to my fingertips. "Or where." The barrel of the gun brushes against my clit, and I cry out.

The tip of his knife circles around each of my breasts, making every hair on my body stand on end. I can't think about anything else, can't control the reaction my body is having while he plays me like a violin. Each new string he plucks elicits a different pitch from my mouth.

The barrel of the gun presses against my lips. "Suck."

"Remove the blindfold and I will."

"You know better than to disobey me." He presses the gun against my mouth harder, clacking against my teeth and wrenching my jaw open.

The metallic taste brushes against my tongue as he thrusts the barrel into my mouth over and over. I gurgle when he pushes it too far and finally pops the gun out of my mouth, a trail of saliva hitting my bare chest. My jaw already aches.

"That's my good girl."

The warmth of his presence leaning over me disappears, and I panic, not knowing what he's going to do next.

Until a cool kiss of air brushes against my pussy.

I gasp, and he continues blowing on me while resting the gun and knife on my thigh. Part of me wants him to use his mouth. Another part of me—a part that must still be delirious from the sedative he gave me—wants him to use that gun and knife.

He kisses my clit and flicks it with his tongue, making me writhe until he replaces his mouth with the handle of the knife. The end presses against my clit, and he wiggles it slowly back and forth, drawing a low moan from my throat.

Jesus. What the hell is wrong with me? How did I go from a boring, celibate, assistant professor to a captive who allows her stalker to make her come with his weapons?

I'm not sure if I'm just as crazy as Saint or crazier.

"You like my knife on your swollen, throbbing clit, don't you, muse?" His voice is distorted by the mask, slipped back into place.

"Yes," I breathe. There's no point in me denying it when he can clearly see and feel the evidence right in front of him.

"Do you think you'll love my gun in your pussy just as much?"

I stiffen. "Wait—"

But the tip of the barrel nudges at my entrance again, still slick with my saliva. "You said you know how to handle a gun. Let's find out how true that is."

"Don't put your fucking gun inside me," I snap.

"Or what?" he purrs. "You'll come all over it?"

I grit my teeth knowing he's right. "Or I'll knee you in the balls once I get out of these restraints."

"Then perhaps I'll keep you tied here forever."

No wonder he blindfolded me. If looks could kill, he'd be dead. "You ass—"

Without warning, Saint pushes the barrel of his gun into my pussy. I cry out at the stretch, the barrel hard and unforgiving. At the same time, the pressure from the butt of the knife on my clit increases, and tears pool at the confusing and overwhelming mix of pleasure and pain.

Saint keeps the gun still as the handle of the knife continues to work me, and the pain from the stretch quickly subsides and gives way to pleasure.

In awe, he murmurs, "My little sinner." Like it's the highest level of praise.

My thighs relax as his words and awestruck tone take their effect, my praise kink making me want to earn more from his lips.

Saint pulls the gun back a little, but keeps it inside me, thrusting the barrel into me once more. I drop my head back and moan. I'm done fighting. I allow the pleasure to consume me.

"How does that feel, muse?" Saint pushes the gun inside me again, the suction of my soaked pussy around the gun turning obscene.

"Amazing," I gasp. "You're going to make me come."

"That's all I ever want. To hear your cries of ecstasy. To make you lose your mind on my tongue, my fingers, my cock, my gun."

The knife handle presses down harder, making my vision go

dark as he thrusts the gun faster inside me. My heart pounds so hard, I would believe him if he told me he could hear it.

"Saint—" I warn, just before the orgasm unexpectedly crashes over me.

I scream as he pounds the gun into me, the knife handle wriggling wildly over my aching, pulsing clit.

Sweat coats my naked skin as wave after wave threatens to drown me in ecstasy.

His murmurs of praise are drowned out by my cries and the buzzing in my ears.

At last, Saint removes the blindfold. His mask fills my vision, his bare biceps flexed as he braces his hands on the arms of my chair. The sight makes my pussy clench. God, every inch of him is perfection.

He removes the mask, finally revealing the glinting irises and the smirk I knew would be awaiting me.

"And what," I pant, "lesson was that?"

"To teach you how to control your fear when you're in real danger." His voice is smooth as silk. "And how to relinquish your control when you're with me."

CHAPTER EIGHT

SAINT

IN THE CORNER OF HIS RAMSHACKLE COTTAGE, THE groundskeeper is on the verge of wetting himself.

By my side, Briar shifts uncomfortably, a pistol concealed on her hip. Hopefully, neither of us will need to resort to violence, but she has the option to defend herself should the worst occur.

"I'm so sorry!" the groundskeeper wails, trembling.

His stringy, greasy hair hangs in his face, gnarly hands dotted in liver spots. His lanky, frail frame leads me to believe he doesn't have the capacity to break into my home, let alone chase anyone through it. But I learned long ago that monsters hide in plain sight. Not to mention he's already repenting for his sins.

"Why did you do it?" My roar could bring down his derelict cottage.

Beside me, Briar flinches as the man cowers. She took one look at him and decided he was innocent.

"I'm sorry!" He holds up his hands in surrender. "I had a bad fall. I haven't been able to get up that mountain, and I didn't think the graves needed tending until spring."

Briar and I both freeze. "Wait. What are you talking about?" I demand.

His wide eyes dart between us. "The-the cemetery. That's

why you're here, isn't it? I'm supposed to be up there taking care of it, I know—"

I hold up my hand to silence his blubbering. "You haven't been up to Nicholson Manor since autumn?"

He shakes his head, skin ghostly. "N-no, I'm sorry—"

"So you didn't try to kill me?" Briar cuts in.

The groundskeeper blanches. "No! No, why would I—no! I would . . . I would never—"

"You didn't break into Nicholson Manor?"

He flinches at my sharp tone. "No! D-did someone break in?" His round gaze flashes to Briar. "Are you all right?"

"I'm fine." She manages a small, tight smile at him before tugging on my arm and murmuring, "Let's go."

Clearly, this man doesn't have a vendetta against my muse and likely couldn't chase her even if he wanted to. My assumptions about his predilection for corpses may have been wrong, but I won't take any chances. "You should know I'll be increasing my security measures around the estate."

The groundskeeper nods enthusiastically. "That's great! That'll deter whoever might've done it. If they come back."

Briar pales, and I grit my teeth. I'm trying to convince her to stay and he's convincing her that whoever chased her through our home could return. "Our apologies for . . . intruding." I nod at his leg before heading for the door. "We hope for your swift recovery."

"Thank you—"

I slam the door behind us.

"Oh my god," Briar hisses as we rush back to my car, harsh winter air piercing through our thick coats and gloves. "How many times have you terrorized that poor man? He was about to shit himself."

"Never. Other than suspecting he possesses a desire for corpses, I've always been on good terms with him."

Briar smacks my arm. "But you thought he was capable of breaking into your manor and trying to kill me?"

I shrug. "Anyone is capable of anything, Briar. There is only one person in this entire world that I know inside and out."

"You don't know *everything* about me," she argues as I open the passenger's side door for her.

"If I don't yet, then I will," I promise. "We have a lifetime together to learn."

She rolls her eyes but smiles before sliding into the car. No sarcastic retort leaves her lips.

She's nearly given herself over to me entirely.

Back at Nicholson Manor, Briar leads the way to the sunroom, where she proofreads the query letter I sent her while I check my email for Zayden's notes on my manuscript.

"There!" She smacks a button on her keyboard. "It's perfect. The spreadsheet is finished too. It has twenty agents listed. From what I can tell, they *might* be good enough to represent you."

From my seat beside her, I brush a strand of silky hair behind her ear, allowing my fingertips to trace down her neck. Goosebumps prick up along her skin. "Why are you helping me?"

Her throat bobs. "Because S.T. Nicholson deserves someone who really believes in him and his work. And I want more books."

So this is about my author persona. The anonymous masked man she still insists on separating from my true identity.

"And," she adds, biting her lip, "you've been through enough shit in your life. I want to do something to make your life better the way you've done for me."

A lump forms in my throat. I wasn't sure this day would ever come. That my muse would want to reciprocate the love and affection I've shown her. That she would someday see me as someone other than her enemy. "You owe me nothing."

"You killed the disgusting predator who was making my life miserable." Her lips curl in revulsion at the memory of Professor Molester. "The least I can do is get you a great agent and a book deal."

Even if she's still guarding her heart, Briar cares about me. That's all I want.

But if I force her to stay here, if I tie her up and lock her away, she may change her mind.

The thought of parting with her, of allowing her to walk out that door, makes fire singe my veins. Our final days of the writing retreat are upon us. If I can't convince her to stay now, she'll leave, and she may never return.

My hand caresses her jaw. "We don't need to return to Auburn. I can support us financially. You can write and no longer worry about work. You'll have everything you need. You'll want for nothing."

Her eyes flutter briefly shut. As if she wants to bask in those words and believe her dream life can become a reality. "No, I need to go back. I have Mack and Cookie and Mom and a job. I can't just up and leave."

Pain twists in my stomach. "You can bring them with you. You saw how many rooms I have."

"I made a commitment to the university," she insists. "And I want to do the job."

I've failed. I left Briar alone, exposed and vulnerable, and now she doesn't want to stay. Too afraid that whoever is out there will return. That I won't be able to keep her safe. That even the job and life that don't make her truly happy are better than being here with me. "And if I refuse to let you go?"

Her fiery blue gaze meets mine. "Then I'll never forgive you. I'd certainly never love you."

The sharp words find their target, spearing my heart. She knew exactly what to say to retain her free will. "You love it here, don't you? With me?"

Briar bites her lip, unable to confess to the truth but incapable of denying it either. "I . . . I do."

Someday, I'll hear those words from her at the altar. "You don't love your job, Briar. You love writing. You love books. But you've been guarding your heart your entire life, refusing to go after what you love out of fear."

"I'm not afraid," she bites, but we both know she's lying.

She's terrified. Terrified of pursuing a career in publishing because she fears how much failure would break her heart. Terrified of loving me, of giving her heart to me for fear of what I'll do with it.

"Take a leap, Briar. This retreat doesn't have to end now. This can be the rest of your life."

A small smile flickers across her lips, and my heart leaps with hope. "I want to at least take my students on the writing retreat and see this next semester through."

My jaw ticks, but I can't force her. Not if I want her heart to be mine. "Fine. But after the semester is over, you'll be back up here with me."

Briar leans toward me, vibrant blue eyes piercing mine. "Because I want to be, not because you forced me."

"So you do?" I murmur. "Want to be here with me?"

Her brows lift in surprise at my vulnerability. "Saint, no man has ever whisked me away for a writing retreat. No man has ever even taken an interest in my writing or my books—two of the things I love most in this world. No man has ever sent me a book off my wishlist, let alone *every* goddamn book. No man has ever watched over me like you or taught me how to protect myself. No man has ever believed in me like you have or . . . loved me like you have. You've killed for me. You've risked everything to be with me. So as insane as it makes me . . . yes. I want to come back and be here. With you."

Even with a thousand years over a thousand lifetimes, I'd never be able to write sweeter words.

CHAPTER NINE
BRIAR

The final days of our writing retreat pass without incident. Despite Saint's presence and my new ability to shoot a bullet through somebody's skull, my paranoia is at an all-time high.

Which is why I'm surprised to find myself mourning the end of our retreat. Getting to throw myself wholly into my writing and emerge only when I want food or a bath or sex has been a dream. Not to mention Saint let me proofread S.T. Nicholson's latest manuscript before he starts sending the query letter to literary agents. This is his best book yet, and I'm not sure if it's because he wrote this book for me or about me.

Aside from the crazed lunatic prowling around, this whole trip has been one of the best months of my life. All of it spent with my psychotic stalker who is surprisingly less psychotic than I ever imagined. Or maybe I'm simply falling for that part of him too.

Still, I'm eager to get home and not be on edge anymore, waiting with bated breath for some assailant to chase me through this giant manor again and catch me this time. Maybe when we return after next semester, they'll be gone for good.

Today, I've taken the day off from writing and holed up in

Saint's library, devouring some of the books he bought me before skimming my finger along the spines of the tomes in his massive collection.

This is the largest home library I've ever seen, complete with a balcony and more bookshelves on the second floor. His shelves are so tall, he's installed a rolling ladder. This is by far my favorite room in Nicholson Manor.

Saint bursts in, finding me admiring his collection. He runs over and sweeps me up, a grin spread wide across his face. "Zayden got his notes back to me. He said it's the best thing I've ever written." He pulls me down by the back of the head for a deep, tender kiss. "Thank you."

I laugh, enchanted by his enthusiasm and unabashed joy. "For what?"

"For being my muse. For being the reason I was able to write again, let alone finish my book. I was on the verge of giving up entirely. I thought I was broken, but you put me back together."

I stroke my hands through his soft, dark hair. My heart squeezes at the pure happiness and adoration lighting up his face. "I didn't do anything other than exist, but you're welcome."

"Your existence is the greatest gift I've ever received." The wide smile travels all the way to his eyes. Since I agreed to return to Nicholson Manor with him, he's been happier than I've ever seen him. "So how would you like to spend the final day of your writing retreat?"

I contemplate his question for a second. "I want to spend it writing for each other. Not manuscripts or other projects, but stories or scenes that we write specifically for the other person. Then we'll read them aloud to each other."

Saint's wicked grin matches my own. He knows exactly what kind of scenes I'm talking about. I couldn't hope for anything better.

We spend the next hour writing the filthiest smut we can come up with, taking turns reading each other's material out loud and giggling. Arousal pools in my belly, panties growing damp. The way his words have always affected me, even before I knew he was the author.

When Saint finishes reading my next scene, he can't restrain himself any longer. He sweeps me up in his arms, carries me to the second floor of his library, and sets my ass on the railing. The banister is wide, but my heart still plummets when I realize how far I could fall with a single wrong move.

He knows exactly what I like. Pleasure mixed with a little bit of danger.

Saint kneels between my legs, hands gripping firmly on my hips. "Do you trust me, Briar?"

That's what he wants most from me. Not my mouth, not my pussy, not even my heart. He wants my trust.

The one gift I'm not sure I'll ever be able to give him.

"I trust you not to fucking drop me. So don't make me regret that."

He manages a small smile. Not exactly the answer he wanted to hear but enough to satisfy him for now.

I dig my nails into the wooden railing when his hand drifts between my thighs, the other still anchoring me in place. He hooks a finger through my panties, pulling them to the side to bare my pussy to him.

He strokes his nose up me first, breathing me in and practically salivating when his eyes fall shut. He lets out a shuddering breath. "You were meant for me, muse. Every inch."

Every time this man opens his mouth, I fall a little bit harder. "No, I'm pretty sure every inch of you was built for me."

He smirks. "We were made for each other."

Before I can say another word, he shuts me up with a stroke of his tongue along my pussy. My eyes roll when he reaches my clit and I start to tip back before remembering I could plummet twenty feet to the ground and I catch myself.

"I'm not letting you go anywhere," Saint murmurs.

His tongue laps at my pussy again, and I clamp my thighs around his head, biting down hard on my lip but unable to stop the loud moan from escaping. I repeat his words from the other night back to him. "This is a library. You need to keep me quiet."

"This is my library. I decide when you need to be quiet and when you can be loud."

"Then make me be loud."

His low chuckle vibrates against my clit. "You'll regret that."

Without another word, he sucks my sensitive nub into his mouth while his finger slides into my pussy, curling to hit that sweet spot.

I cry out, thighs already shaking with the mounting pleasure.

"You're coming on my mouth and then on my cock," he growls like a warning.

"What if I can't come twice?" I taunt, knowing very well that Saint can easily wring two orgasms from my body in quick succession.

"I've got all night," he purrs.

I'll have to add that to my bucket list. An all-nighter with Saint de Haas.

He sucks my clit deep, thrusting his finger hard until he slips in a second, the stretch making me groan.

Pleasure mounts in my limbs along with the panic that I won't be able to control my shuddering, trembling body once the orgasm hits, and I'll go tumbling over the edge. Somehow, the spike of terror and adrenaline makes the orgasm come on faster.

Waves of pleasure rocket through me as I come on his mouth and fingers, clawing at him and crying out as my thighs shake uncontrollably. His hand on my hip clamps around me, pinning me in place.

Before I've recovered from the orgasm, he stands, yanking me down and spinning me so I'm facing away from him. He lifts my feet off the ground, bending me over the railing.

I yelp, the floor far below me, making my stomach flip. "Saint! Put me down!"

But he ignores my pleas. "Grab onto the chandelier," he commands.

The chandelier dangling from the ceiling is mere inches from my fingertips now. "I'll break it and fall!"

"I don't give a fuck if you break it," he growls. "And I'm not going to let you fall. If you trust me, you'll let me fuck you like this, muse."

"Don't make me use our safe word," I snap.

"You're welcome to use it anytime. That's what it's for. Now hang onto the chandelier."

Against every instinct in my body, I release my death grip on the railing and reach for the chandelier.

Behind me, Saint holds me steady with a hand on my hip and his body pinning my pelvis against the railing.

When he slides inside me, the abrupt stretch makes me cry out. "Agh!"

"Don't let go, muse!" he shouts before ramming into me.

His cock fills every inch of me, making my pussy throb and weep for him. Both of his hands are clamped around my hips now, keeping my ass against him as it bounces back against his torso with every hard thrust. Above our heads, the chandelier rattles violently, and I brace myself for the second the chains holding it up will give out.

My pussy is already aching, sore after fucking Saint multiple times a day. With the tension in every muscle, my walls are clenched around his cock tighter than usual. "I'm sore. I can't go much longer."

"You're going to have to waddle then, muse. I'm not even close."

I grit my teeth, grip tightening on the chandelier as I'm unable to do anything other than let Saint pound me against the railing. Completely and utterly at his mercy.

"I can be faster if you come," he pants. "You know how hard and fast I come when you scream my name."

I love that nothing makes him come harder than my own release.

He leans his weight against me, making my arms shake and struggle to hang onto the chandelier. "Show me how much you love getting fucked by me. Squeeze that pussy on my cock."

I cry out, doing as I'm told, clenching on his cock as hard as I can, hoping that's enough to make him finish sooner. "I want you to come inside me."

"I can't give it to you until you come on my cock, muse." He slams into me so hard and deep, his balls slap against my pussy. "Oh, fuck! Briar!"

With my name on his lips, overwhelming pleasure pulses through me and my scream echoes in the library, my grip on the chandelier slipping. It rocks violently over our heads, and my heart leaps to my throat as I start to fall forward. My screams of ecstasy turn to screams of terror, but Saint catches me by the hair, holding my torso up and keeping my hips pinned against the railing while he continues fucking me wildly.

The pleasure is too much, sparklers firing off in my brain. "Saint!" I scream.

He roars at his name leaving my lips, slamming into me twice more before spilling inside me. I yelp with every hard jerk of his cock deep inside my pussy.

His cock slowly slides out of me, taking a rush of cum with him before he peels our sticky bodies apart. We're both panting, my heart slamming against my ribcage harder than when a madman was chasing me.

"Thank you for not letting me fall," I pant.

I can't believe we just did that. That was reckless and stupid and dangerous and utterly euphoric. Every time I think I've had the best sex of my life, Saint de Haas blows my mind again.

He presses a heartbreakingly tender kiss against my lips. "I told you you can trust me. I'll only ever let you fall for me."

CHAPTER TEN
SAINT

Though Briar will never trust me if I lock her in Nicholson Manor and prevent her from leaving, it takes every ounce of willpower to let her go. To watch her hips and ass sway as she strides out those doors before I drive her back to her house.

Our writing retreat was supposed to be enough. Supposed to be enough to convince her to stay with me. To never leave my side.

Now every second she's not with me, I'll be worrying about where she is. Who she's with. Who's watching her. Who's waiting for his chance to hurt her.

Maybe if I hadn't made the mistake of leaving her at Nicholson Manor alone, maybe if I had been there to kill the intruder who chased her through my own home, she would've been willing to stay. She would've witnessed with her own eyes the lengths I'm willing to go to in order to protect her.

When I pull into her driveway, a man with salt and pepper hair and a slight hunch to his shoulders is seated on her porch steps.

My hands grip the steering wheel hard enough to tear it

from the dashboard. Is this the motherfucker who was chasing her through Nicholson Manor?

He's gotten bolder. Waiting for her outside her own fucking house in broad daylight.

I'll rip his head off.

As we come to a stop, he stands and I finally get a clear view of his face.

Fuck.

That can't fucking be him—

But it is.

Warren Marshall.

I should've known he'd be the one behind this.

Briar glowers at him, and before I can stop her from getting out of the car, she shoves her door open. "Dad? What the hell are you doing here?"

Dad?

Dad.

No. No, there's no fucking way Warren Marshall is—

But the man who approaches Briar with a wary smile is missing an ear.

An ear that's safely stored with my other trophies.

Cecilia Shea never took her husband's last name. She kept her maiden name and passed it on to their only child—Briar.

Briar is Warren Marshall's daughter.

Daughter of the man who murdered my mother.

My heart has never pounded so hard in my life. Any second now, it'll burst.

Both of them turn as I slowly exit my car.

This could be a mistake. Perhaps I should be peeling out of the driveway and speeding as far away from this monster as I can get. But I won't leave Briar alone with him.

Warren hasn't tracked me down since I took his ear. But that doesn't mean he hasn't tried.

His brows descend low over his beady eyes. The same shade

of blue as Briar's, but without the sunlight hers hold. His are the hard, dangerous blue of ice. He steps between me and my muse.

His second mistake.

"How did you find out where I live?" Briar demands.

"Your mother told me." He points at the house without diverting his gaze from me. "Briar, get inside."

She folds her arms defiantly across her chest. "I'm not going anywhere. I'd like *you* to leave, actually."

"This man is dangerous." Fire blazes in Warren's eyes. "You need to get away from him now."

Her gaze darts between us. She doesn't deny that I'm dangerous. That would be pointless. "How the hell do you know Saint?"

Warren grabs Briar's shoulder in an attempt to guide her into the house.

"Take your hands off her."

He balks at my order just long enough for Briar to jerk out of his grasp. "Both of you, inside," she barks. We both start to object until she points at the door and shouts, "Now!"

The last place Warren Marshall and I should be is alone together in the privacy of Briar's home. I'll paint her walls crimson with his blood if I must.

Reluctantly, I follow them inside. I never thought I'd see this monster again, and now here he is.

My future father-in-law.

The monster who killed my mother is also my muse's deadbeat father. Now, he's in her house. He'll be at our wedding. If he survives to see that day.

One word from Briar and I'll make sure Warren Marshall never takes another breath.

Inside, tension permeates through every square foot of Briar's home. My muse examines us with hands on her hips and lowered brows. "What the hell is the proper etiquette in this situation? Am I supposed to offer you a seat and some tea? Coffee?"

"He won't be staying," I tell her, just as Warren grumbles, "Coffee."

"Sit," Briar orders. Warren takes a seat at one end of her too-short, rickety table and I take a seat at the other. Briar rolls her eyes before brewing coffee and settling into the chair between us.

"Well." I examine Warren with the disdain of an introvert who's received unexpected company. "You've aged horribly."

"How the hell do you know each other?" Briar demands.

Warren glares at me wordlessly. He doesn't want his daughter to know his true nature. Maybe he also wants to spare her from knowing mine.

He's far too late for that.

I reach for one of Briar's fists on the table, uncurling it to slide my fingers through hers. Warren's jaw ticks. "Remember when I told you about the man whose ear I removed?"

Slowly, the puzzle pieces click together in Briar's head until her eyes widen and snap to her father. "You said you lost your ear in a dog attack."

He pales before sputtering, "He's lying."

Her eyes narrow. "He's always honest. *You're* the liar."

She has him there. I've been honest with her from day one —I've confessed to the sacrifices I've made for her, the lives I've taken, the painful parts of my past I never disclose to anyone. But she's always known him to be secretive, disloyal, deceptive.

Warren sighs. "Of course I couldn't tell you the truth."

"You *killed* a woman! A little boy's mom." Briar's voice cracks on the final words. She can feel the pain I experienced as if it's her own. God, I love her so much.

And though she's not yet ready to admit it, though she may not even be aware of it herself, she's falling deeply in love with me.

Warren slams a fist down on the table, shaking it. "After she killed my brother! Your uncle!"

"Because he tried molesting her son!"

Her father's jaw clenches to the verge of snapping. "He wasn't like that."

Figures he would also be the sort of bastard who defends a child predator, even in death.

"A woman doesn't kill a man because she *didn't* catch him trying to molest her son." Briar's cheeks are rosy now.

My eyes prick not from the painful memories but from the fierceness in Briar's tone. Her protectiveness.

A woman who once despised me, who wanted me out of her life forever, is now defending me to her own father. Choosing me.

I squeeze her hand. "My mother didn't kill your brother." Both of them fall silent, gazes landing on me. "I did."

"You?" Warren barks. "You couldn't have. You would've been just a child."

"Yes. To your brother's delight."

Warren's mouth twists into a snarl. "I don't want you anywhere near my daughter."

"You don't get a say in who I spend my time with anymore," Briar snaps. "In fact, you don't get a say in any part of my life. I literally don't even want you in my house."

He whirls on her. "He doesn't give a shit about you, Briar! He's here for me. You think this is a coincidence? He killed my brother, I killed his mother, and now he's planning to kill you." His gaze lasers back on me. "But he'll have to go through me first."

A flash of fear in Briar's wide, bright blue irises.

She slips her hand from mine.

My heart plummets to my feet. She can't possibly believe his vile accusations. Not after everything we've been through. Everything I've already done for her to prove my love, my eternal devotion.

She's agreed to return to Nicholson Manor with me. To live with me, be with me. I can't lose her already.

"Don't listen to him, Briar. He's hurt you countless times. I would never, *ever* hurt you. You know that."

Trust. That's what I still need from her. Her full, unwavering trust. But I'm not yet sure I've earned it.

With her watery blue eyes trained on me, she gives a single nod. "I know."

Relief floods through me. She won't let him get in her head. She knows the real me.

I haven't lost her.

"Get out," Warren orders.

I stand and head for the door. If I don't leave, I'll tear his head from his body, and I'm not sure Briar would forgive me for that.

If anyone deserves to kill him, it's her.

CHAPTER ELEVEN

BRIAR

"Oh my god! How was the sex?"

I snort. Of course this would be the most important information Mack needs to know first. "Amazing. Best-sex-of-my-life kind of amazing."

She squeals, scooting closer on the couch. "I knew it! Wow. Okay, and how was everything else? You like being with him? He treats you well?"

"Better than any man ever has," I admit. In my lap, Cookie purrs. After a can of tuna, she's finally stopped giving me the cold shoulder for abandoning her with Mack for a month.

"I'm still trying to come to terms with the fact that you didn't tell me about your secret relationship and that you've been having the best sex of your life, and now you know your father killed his mom."

"Yeah, my life is fucking insane right now. I'm sorry I didn't tell you sooner. I wasn't sure what you'd think, and I didn't want to hear you say you told me so about all that love shit."

"*Love?*" she practically screeches. "You *love* him?"

My heart thuds, realizing too late what I've just admitted out loud to my best friend who will never, ever let me live this down.

"I mean, I'm not *in love* with him. I haven't known him that long."

"You've known him for months. And it sounds like you've been spending a lot of time together that you didn't tell me about. That's plenty of time to fall in love with someone. Especially if he's giving you the best orgasms of your life."

Maybe Mack is right, but I won't admit that out loud. I can't.

"Wow. *Your* father killed *his* mother."

I sigh. "Yes. This is the fifth time you've said it, and it's still true."

Mack shakes her head, dumbstruck. She stares up at the ceiling like that will give her all the answers. "I just can't wrap my mind around it."

"How do you think I feel?"

"What did Saint say?"

"That's the worst part." I bite my lip. "He stormed out."

My father killed Saint's mother. He turned an already traumatized boy into an orphan. Saint's mother was the only person he had in the entire world, the only one who loved him, and my father took her away.

If I thought what my father did to my mother was unforgivable, what he did to Saint is a thousand times worse. Not to mention my uncle was apparently a child predator. My stomach churns at the thought of their DNA coursing through my veins. I wish I could cut them out of my family tree like tumors.

Saint will never be able to love me after this. The moment he stormed out the door is probably the last I'll ever see of him. Who could love someone born from a monster like that? I'm the spawn of the man responsible for ruining his life.

"Do you think your dad was right? About Saint coming after you for revenge? Obviously, he's not now. He totally would've killed you by now if that was the case. Or in front of your dad."

I shake my head. "No, he was never after me for revenge.

He'd never hurt me. And he was genuinely shocked when he met my dad and realized who he is."

I still haven't wrapped my head around it. I knew my father was a cheating asshole, but I never suspected he'd be capable of murder. Saint was right—anyone is capable of anything. Everything I know about my father barely scratches the surface of who he really is.

"Do you think . . ." Mack chews on her lip. "Do you think your dad might try to do something to Saint? To keep him away from you?"

I snort. "He's in his sixties now and he looks like shit. If he tries going after Saint, he has a death wish." My father had years to get revenge on him for taking his ear. Maybe he decided they were even. At least until he spotted Saint with me. "But he might not have to keep Saint away from me anyway."

Mack's brows fold together. "What do you mean?"

"My father killed his mom, Mack. He's not just going to forgive me for what my family did to him. They ruined his childhood. They took away the only person who ever mattered to him."

Mack grabs my hand and squeezes. "Yeah, *they* did that, not you. He won't hold you responsible for what your family did. He just needs time to process and cool down."

God, I hope she's right. Minus the crazy psycho who watched us fuck and chased me through Nicholson Manor, our writing retreat was one of the best months of my life. As crazy as it is, I'm falling for my stalker, and I'm not ready for this thing between us to be over.

My phone buzzes with a call from an unknown number. Four missed calls. Probably my psycho-killer father trying to justify his actions and worm his way back into my life. I haven't needed him for years, and I certainly don't need him now. Especially if his presence drives Saint away.

"Aren't you going to answer that?" Mack asks when my phone rings again.

"It's probably just my father."

"What if somebody's going into labor?"

"Like who?"

"I don't know—it could be a wrong number and they won't realize they're not calling Grandma until you answer."

I huff through my nose and answer the call. "Sorry, I think you have the wrong number."

To my surprise, no one responds.

"Hello?"

More silence.

"Dad? Are you there?"

Seriously? This asshole is going to blow up my phone and then not even have the decency to respond? "I thought the era of prank calls was over. Don't you have better shit to do with your time?"

Still, they say nothing.

"Is your phone on mute or something? Hit the mute button."

Silence.

Maybe this isn't my father at all. He definitely wouldn't shut up if he'd gotten me to answer his call. "Is this one of those creepy phone sex fetish things? They have hotlines for this. Go call one of them." I hang up. "Why is life being such a bitch?"

Mack stands. "I'm going to pour us some wine."

"It's the middle of the afternoon," I call as she retreats into the kitchen.

"Exactly! That's why I said wine, not liquor."

My phone screen lights up again. A call from the same number. You've got to be kidding me.

"You better say something this time."

When I'm greeted with more silence, I nearly scream. This is already the most aggravating conversation I've ever had, and they still haven't said a word.

What if this is about Austin? Or Dr. Barrett? Somebody who

knows that I was involved somehow. Someone who wants to avenge one of their deaths. And they think I'm their target.

Maybe that blonde girl who was following me in the black BMW.

"Whatever you think you know about me, you're wrong. Don't call me again."

As soon as I hang up, I block the number and call Trevor.

"Hey, Briar! Are you back home? How was the retreat?" His jolly, familiar voice actually gives me an ounce of comfort.

"Do you think you could trace a phone number for me?"

The cheeriness in his tone morphs to confusion. "Possibly. I can ask my buddy down at the station."

"Thank you. Let me text it to you. And before you ask, yes, I already blocked the number."

"What's this all about?"

"I kept getting repeat calls from an unknown number like somebody was on fire, but when I finally answered, they refused to say anything. I'd dismiss it as some stupid prank, but something crazy happened on my writing retreat."

"What happened?" Trevor asks, more urgent now.

"I'm fine," I reassure him. "But I thought I saw someone watching me through the window one night. And then there was another night that the power went out, and someone broke in. I know they're probably not connected at all, but—"

"Wait, Briar. Someone was lurking outside watching you through a window, broke into your house, and now you're getting calls from a mysterious stranger? This has to be your stalker."

I shake my head, even though he can't see me. "No. This isn't Saint."

He was with me inside Nicholson Manor when I saw the stranger lurking outside, but I can't tell Trevor that.

"How do you know? You saw their face?"

"No," I admit. "But I know this isn't him."

Trevor's voice is full of skepticism now. "How?"

"I know where he was when the intruder was watching me and when they broke in. The intruder couldn't have been him."

"And what about the calls? How do you know he isn't calling you from a new number?"

"They're silent. That's not his MO."

Saint hasn't been silent since that first night he lingered outside my house in a mask. Besides, what reason could he possibly have to call me from a different number?

"Maybe his MO is messing with your head," Trevor suggests gently. I know he's only trying to be a voice of reason, and maybe if I didn't know Saint as well as I do and I had a rational brain cell left in my head, I'd agree with him. "I'll see what I can do about getting the number traced."

A relieved sigh unravels the tight knot in my chest. "Thank you."

Before Trevor hangs up, he adds, "Just . . . don't trust him, okay?"

I nearly tell him I'm struggling with the exact opposite problem. I'm not sure I'll ever fully trust Saint, or anybody. "I won't."

CHAPTER TWELVE
SAINT

WHEN WARREN MARSHALL SHUFFLES INTO THE DIMLY LIT lobby of the hotel, I wave him over to the plush armchairs. Other than the receptionist behind the desk, we're alone.

He stops in his tracks, not particularly eager to be in my presence again. I crook a finger at him. Too bad he doesn't have a choice.

Warren approaches reluctantly, glancing around for witnesses. He should know I'm smart enough not to kill a man somewhere so public. At least not when I'm without my mask.

With a sigh, he lowers himself into the plush armchair across from me, a low coffee table with magazines scattered across its surface between us. More like a dentist's waiting room than a hotel lobby.

The single ear he has left is droopy, flaring out from his skull and dotted with liver spots. Warren takes in our surroundings again before leaning forward. "What do you want?"

"You're wrong about me." I adjust the stiff shirt cuff around my wrist. "Unlike you, I have no intentions of hurting Briar. Or of leaving her. If I intended to kill her, you'd already be planning her funeral."

Warren's mouth curdles in disgust. "That supposed to make me feel better?"

"If I were a father, it would certainly reassure me to know the man betrothed to my daughter loves her unconditionally."

His skin pales. "You're engaged?"

"Soon to be." I sit forward, elbows on my knees. "As far as I'm concerned, our history is buried. I'm willing to move past it and allow you to continue living for Briar's sake if you're willing to do the same."

Warren scoffs, leaning back and averting his gaze, even though he knows my offer is the best he could hope for.

I shrug and lean back. "Otherwise, if you want to kill me, you might as well do it now."

Warren is well past his prime. A feeble old man who hasn't bothered to take care of himself well enough to remain independent and healthy for much longer. He is a man with little to lose but without the strength he would need to defend himself against me, and he knows I'm not going down without a fight.

A full three minutes of silence tick by before Warren finally clears his throat. "My daughter may not realize it, but she's the most important person in my life. I want to move forward. Make amends for my past."

"If you intend to make amends with Briar, you're already too late." My muse has long since decided to cut her father out of her life. I will do nothing to stand in her way, even if she has a miraculous change of heart.

"I am well aware of my daughter's resentment toward me. I don't expect her forgiveness. At this point, I only wish for her safety and happiness."

"We're in agreement there." Perhaps the only thing Warren Marshall and I will ever agree on, the only common ground we'll find—Briar. His daughter. My muse.

Her family ripped me apart, but she put me back together. A devious twist of fate.

Warren assesses me. "Is it true, what you said earlier? You're the one who stabbed my brother?"

"Yes. Don't ask me if I regret it."

"Because the answer would be no?" A rhetorical question. He doesn't need the answer. We both know I could never regret taking the life of the man who attempted to hurt me and kill my mother. "I'm assuming you still have my ear as well."

"Do you want it back? I can't imagine it looks much better than the one you have remaining."

He leans back in the chair, drumming his fingers on the armrest. "So you intend to propose to my daughter?"

"I will. When the timing is right."

He snorts. "*If* she agrees—"

"Don't bother with a speech about how I need to treat your daughter when you have no idea how to do so yourself."

The sharp edge in my tone silences him.

I took his brother; he took my mother. We both lost someone we cared about. What's done is done. He can continue to come after me, but that will only worsen his relationship with Briar. She already hates him. If he kills me, she may just seek revenge on her own father.

I did teach her how to shoot, after all.

Warren stands, nodding once. "Keep the ear. And be good to my daughter."

I flash him a grin. "I'll be a saint."

CHAPTER THIRTEEN
BRIAR

On campus, the administration temporarily gives me Dr. Barrett's old office, and I reorganize the entire room and burn sage to get rid of any bad spirits. His ghost is likely well aware that I know exactly who killed him.

This morning, I received a text from a different unknown number.

> Aren't you supposed to be preparing for class?

I've never believed in ghosts, but I'm starting to think Dr. Barrett's vengeful ass is haunting me. I'll have to Google whether ghosts can interact with technology, but I'm going to guess they can.

> Pretty blue dress today. Wearing it for someone special?

The hairs on the back of my neck stand up as my body temperature spikes. I drop my gaze, forgetting what I threw on this morning in my rush to get out the door and onto campus in time for my first class.

A navy blue dress paired with leggings.

Three sharp knocks on Dr. Barrett's office door—*my* office door—and when I swing it open, Saint leans against the frame with a smug grin. He's in dark slacks, shiny shoes, and a button-down with a silky blue tie.

"Good morning, Professor," he purrs, not waiting for an invitation before he shuts the door behind him and strides into the room.

Relief floods through me. He doesn't hate me. He's not avoiding me after discovering my family's dark, depraved history.

I throw my arms around him. He chuckles, surprised, before squeezing me in a tight embrace.

"I'm so sorry," I whisper. "My family is fucking nuts." I pull back, not wanting to utter the words but forcing them out anyway. "I understand if you can't be with me anymore."

His onyx eyes narrow. "What are you talking about, muse? Not even death will drive us apart."

His words nearly make me collapse to my knees in relief. "My father killed your mother. My uncle tried to molest you. It would be perfectly reasonable for you to break up with me. That's probably the best reason I've ever heard to break up with someone, actually."

"Warren Marshall is the last person I will allow to come between us. Nothing will take me from you, muse. Nothing."

I can't hold back my grin. Maybe I should've suspected that someone as insane as Saint wouldn't let murder come between us. "Wow, I finally met someone who hates my father more than I do."

"I don't hate him," he says evenly, and I wonder how he can feel that way when even I hate my father. "He avenged someone he loved. I would do the same for you. Though I can't say I won't be delighted once he's gone. How much longer is he going to be in town?"

"I don't know. I haven't heard from him since I told him to get out of my house." Hopefully, I won't see my father ever again.

Saint nods to the sage. "So how's the new office? I see you've been warding off the evil spirits."

"Yes, but it's not working because now they're texting me."

He frowns where he's leaning against my desk as I show him my phone screen.

"What if this is whoever was watching us have sex that night?" I suggest. "What if it's someone tied to Austin or Dr. Barrett? They could believe that I'm responsible. According to the police, I'm the last confirmed person to see either of them alive. A death and a disappearance in a matter of months linked to me doesn't exactly look good."

Saint doesn't miss the resentment in my tone. If it wasn't for him, I wouldn't be in this mess. He takes both of my hands in his. "Nothing is going to happen to you with me around. I'll hunt this person down and make him regret every single instance he ever glanced in your direction."

"Good." I'm already so sick of this shit. The stress is building inside me, and I need something to release it. I slip the straps of my dress down. "Now. Maybe we can break in my new office."

He can provide the distraction I need to forget about this mess. About this new crazy person who has entered my life to chase, harass, and scare me. About my father being back in town —a killer who ruined Saint's life. All of it.

Saint's mouth finds my bare shoulder and gently kisses the skin there. "I seem to recall how wet I made you when I had you on another desk."

My thighs clench at the delicious memory. "It's only right that we christen this one."

Luckily, Dr. Barrett's desk has already been wiped clean of everything but his computer in the corner. Saint grabs me up by the hips and plants me on the desk.

"We have to be quiet," I warn. There are several other people in this faculty building, and I have no idea how thin the walls are.

"You're the one with the volume problems. But if you wish me to keep you quiet, I'll do exactly that." He loosens the tie around his neck.

I trail a finger over the silky length. "Why did you wear a tie? Even for you, this is rather formal."

He grins. "For this exact occasion." Saint sticks a finger past my lips, letting me suck it before he opens my mouth, stuffing the tie inside. "Mmm. Good girl."

I flip him off, but he ignores me, his expert fingers slowly unzipping the back of my dress before pulling down the top and strapless bra, allowing them to pool at my waist. "I'll do whatever it takes to get an A, Professor."

Goosebumps prick up along my arms at his low, seductive tone and the slow, careful way he explores my body like it's his first time ravishing me all over again.

Saint blows on my nipples and they peak beneath his cool breath. He sucks one into his mouth before massaging the other, making me groan around the tie gagging me.

A casual finger strokes up my panties. "Already so wet for me, Professor."

I reach for the tie in my mouth to tell him to stop calling me that, but he smacks my hand back down onto the desk.

He tsks. "We don't want anyone hearing you, do we, Professor? No one can know how hard your student makes you come behind closed doors."

Saint infuriates me almost as much as he turns me on. But I keep my hand glued to the desk as he lifts my dress and trails kisses down my stomach. His tongue swirls around my navel before he nips a path along my pelvis.

Even if I could tell him that I don't have much time before class, he wouldn't listen. If Saint de Haas wants to take his time making me come, that's exactly what he's going to do. Consequences be damned. When we're like this, nothing else in the world exists.

His teeth travel down to my mound, nipping and sinking his teeth into me through the thin fabric of my panties. Whimpers in my throat are lost to the barrier keeping me quiet.

"If I removed the tie from your mouth, would you beg for my tongue?"

I nod quickly. I'll beg every day for that wicked tongue if he tells me to.

That's enough to satisfy him. He draws my panties to the side, the heat of my arousal escaping.

"I can't remember what I lived for before I met you," he murmurs, and I'm not sure if he's talking to me or my pussy.

When his tongue flicks out and makes contact with my clit, I don't care. My eyes roll back, head dropping, as he finally gives me the gratification I'm aching for.

His tongue glides up my pussy once, twice, three times before swirling around my clit. His tongue dances around it, not quite hitting that sensitive, swollen spot. I growl through the tie in my mouth. He loves nothing more than tormenting me. Sadistic fuck.

Saint answers my growl with a throaty chuckle, but he still doesn't give me the pleasure I crave. His tongue strokes back up through the wetness between my legs, my gaze darting to the closed door when the squish of his tongue against my wetness is loud even to my ears. Did we lock the door?

My heart thunders harder at the risk of getting caught with Saint between my legs on my first day of the new semester. He notices the new tension in my legs and my distracted attention because he draws my focus back with a sharp nip on my clit.

My gasp is drowned out by the tie gagging me.

"Eyes on me, muse," he orders. "When my mouth and hands are on you, your attention doesn't stray from me. Ever."

I stare down at him in a challenge, and he meets my glare.

"Yes, even in a fire."

I roll my eyes.

"Get used to flames, muse. There will be a lot where we're headed."

He licks at my sensitive nub to soothe it, drawing a moan from deep in my chest before he finally sucks it between his lips.

I hunch forward, biting down on the gag and nails digging into the edge of the desk.

His finger slides into my pussy with ease, and we both groan, his vibrating my clit.

Saint switches between licking and sucking and nipping at my sensitive nub, frustration mounting in my limbs. I thrust my pussy forward into his mouth, leaving him with no doubts about what I would be communicating with my mouth if not for the tie garbling my words.

"Always so impatient for your release." He slows the thrusting of his finger and I want to kick him. "Someday, you'll learn to accept what I give you, as fast or as slow as I want to give it."

He is the most frustrating, annoying, insufferable—

Saint slides a second finger inside me, emitting a soft groan as I cry out. His dark gaze stays trained on me like I'm the only thing in this room. In the world. "That's it, muse," he breathes. "You're going to come on my fingers before you come on my cock."

He's right. I can't stop the orgasm barreling toward me now. I try to block out the fear of another faculty member opening the door to my new office and finding us here.

Saint's eyes roll when he sucks my clit and a flood of arousal coats his fingers. My clit throbs in his mouth as the orgasm strikes, sending rivulets of pleasure zipping down to my toes.

I cry out around the tie in my mouth, grateful for the gag suppressing the sounds I can't contain. Saint keeps sucking my clit hard, draining me of all energy as my limbs go limp with pleasure.

He pops his fingers out of me and straightens, pulling the damp tie from my mouth and stuffing it back in his pocket.

"Don't worry, muse. My hand will keep you quiet this time. Now bend over."

"I need to get to class—"

Saint spins me, pushing my back down so my bare breasts are pressed against the desk. "You should've thought about that before you spread your legs for me. I'm not leaving until I come inside this sweet pussy."

The clink of his belt unfastening echoes in the office, followed by the purr of his zipper descending. With one hand, he keeps my wrists pinned to my back. With the other, he guides his erection to my entrance.

"Don't let them hear you getting fucked, Professor," he warns before he slams inside me.

I gasp and bite down hard on my lip to suppress my moans, tasting copper.

He keeps my wrists pinned behind my back and brings his other hand around to muffle my moans with his hand. I groan into his palm, my breasts squeaking against the desk with every hard thrust.

Low groans reverberate from his throat. He's far too vocal for public sex.

I wriggle free of his hand on my mouth. "You're going to get us caught," I hiss.

"Then stop clenching your pussy on my cock."

"I'm not!"

He lets out a louder groan then, and I'm certain we're going to be discovered any second.

"Saint!" I warn. "If we get caught, you'll get me fired."

His brows furrow as he continues fucking me. "I'm not forcing my cock inside you. You welcomed me in. It won't be my fault if you get fired—I'm just your impressionable student." He leans down to whisper in my ear, his cock hitting deeper with the new angle. "And if you get fired, I'll just have to whisk you away to Nicholson Manor forever."

I grit my teeth. "Asshole." He knew exactly what he was doing when he entered my office this morning.

His thrusts turn punishing at the insult, pain mixing with the pleasure as his thick cock stretches me.

Part of me wants to tell him to stop, that this stretch is too much, that his hand is doing a shitty job of masking the moans escaping past my lips. But I can't find the words, too desperate to come to care about anything else.

His hand barely muffles my cries as his cock drives me over the edge, sending me tumbling down into the pits of pleasure.

"*Fuck*," he hisses, collapsing on top of me, and riding out my orgasm with every thrust until he slams into me so hard, my vision flickers. "Fuck, Briar!"

Once the final wave of pleasure has ebbed, he yanks me off the desk and shoves me to my knees.

"Open that wicked mouth." His command is tinged with desperation as he pumps his cock in front of my face.

I obey, and he shoves his cock past my lips, coating my tongue with my own arousal before his hard length jerks. Every spurt of cum hits the back of my throat, forcing me to swallow each drop.

I wait for him to pull out so we can desperately tug our clothes back into place, but he remains still, holding my head in place and heaving. "So about that library I promised you," he pants. "Will the library in Nicholson Manor suffice, or will you need a library all of your own?"

At last, he pulls his cock free, allowing me to speak. His salty taste lingers on my tongue and in my throat. "You promised me *you* would write me a library full of books."

He chuckles. "I better get to work then."

I tug my clothes back into place and attempt to fix my hair. "Yes, you should." I clear my throat. "See you in class, Mr. de Haas."

He smirks. "Did I earn my A, Professor?"

"Yes." I shove him toward the door. "Now get out."

My heart hammers when he opens the door, but there are no horrified faces listening in on the other side. Thank god. That was way too risky.

When my phone buzzes, I expect it to be a dirty text from Saint. But it's the same unknown number that texted me earlier.

> Be sure to pick up more milk on the way home. You're all out.

What the fuck? Is this psycho in my house right now? My thumbs fly over the screen.

> Who the hell are you?

> You know exactly who I am.

I take a screenshot and send it to Mack.

> Looks like I have another stalker.

Seconds later, Mack calls me. "What do you mean *another* stalker?"

I explain to her what happened on the writing retreat while tissue paper crinkles in the background as she packs copies of S.T. Nicholson's books for giveaways. "And now they're texting and calling me." My phone buzzes. "Oh, look, another text."

"Don't respond," Mack warns as my thumbs fly over the screen. "You don't want to engage with them. They'll take that as an invitation to keep contacting you."

"Too bad I've already sent off a hearty *fuck you*."

Mack sighs, tearing off a strip of tape. "I'm serious, Briar. Don't engage with them anymore, and keep all of the evidence."

"From now on, I'll do my best to refrain." Whether my best will be enough is another story.

"Why do you think this new person is stalking you?"

I chew on my lip. "I'm not sure. Maybe because of what happened to Austin and Dr. Barrett. Someone thinks I'm responsible. I've seen this blonde woman in a BMW a few times. Saint also mentioned he has enemies. Maybe it's someone from his past retaliating for something."

Whoever it is, they're obviously nothing like Saint. They're not stalking me because they're obsessed and in love with me—they want to hurt me.

"Saint has *enemies*?" Mack hisses. "Is he in the mafia?"

"No! Not that I know of, anyway." I'm sure he would've told me if he was. Pretty sure.

"Good," she says before sighing. "So I guess we have a new stalker to track down."

The Auburn Institute of Fine Arts is holding a vigil tonight in honor of Dr. Barrett. Mack insisted on coming with us once she learned that Saint and I will be in attendance to survey the crowd for my new stalker. If my stalker is hell-bent on avenging Dr. Barrett, they'll undoubtedly be at his vigil. If they're avenging Austin, they'll be here too. For me.

Mack and Saint have been talking business the entire way here. Giveaways and signings and contracts and emails. All of it effectively shutting me out of the conversation entirely. I can't help the annoying prickle of jealousy that flares every time Saint says something that makes Mack laugh.

Warmth crawls up to my chest when I spot Officer Rosario and Officer Smith in the corner, monitoring the attendees just as we are. The same way they'd show up to a funeral to watch for the killer. Smith's gaze narrows on me.

"You should be proud they suspect you," Saint mutters.

80

"They think you're capable of carefully and quietly making a grown man disappear."

"I am capable of that," I purr. "So watch your back."

Saint chuckles.

As soon as I spot Dr. Barrett's wife, Nancy, I take the opportunity to veer away from Saint and Mack. It's hard to believe I didn't even know she existed until the night Dr. Barrett died, but now I could pick her face and voice out of a lineup. She's constantly on the news encouraging people to help look for her missing husband.

Nancy likely isn't my new stalker, but I can't rule her out yet. There are plenty of women her age who commit murder and who knows what the police have told her about their suspicions. If they informed her I'm the last known person to have seen her husband, she may have decided to come after me for more information about where he ended up.

Nancy swallows quickly when she notices me approaching over the rim of her mug. By the flush to her cheeks and her dilated pupils, she definitely doesn't have coffee or tea in that mug. She waves her handkerchief in the air, streaked black with her running mascara.

I hold out my hand. "Hi, I'm Dr. Briar Shea. I worked with your husband."

"Thank you so much for coming." She shakes my hand like I'm made of glass.

"Of course. How are you holding up?" I force out the small talk even though all I want to do is grill her on the investigation and what she's been doing with her time outside of her media appearances.

She sniffles. "Oh, as well as can be expected."

"I hate to ask, but . . ." I lower my voice. "Do the police have any idea where he could be?"

She shakes her head. "They don't have any idea. At least, not that they've shared with me. But I'll tell you my theory." She leans closer, the schnapps pungent on her breath. "I think he left because I was pushing him into retirement. That was his final straw. He's been sick of me for a long time. And I've been sick of him even longer."

The bastard blamed his wife for his delayed retirement when in reality, he was the one who didn't want to stop working. Probably because that would mean fewer opportunities to prey on vulnerable young women.

Nancy takes another swig she doesn't need from her mug. "So he disappeared instead of divorcing me so I can't get half of his shit. To tell you the truth, I'm glad to be rid of him. I know he was whoring around behind my back, but he thought he was so clever and I was just the bimbo he married." A dark chuckle before her fearful gaze flashes to me. "That makes me sound guilty. I swear I didn't do anything to my husband. Thought about it. But didn't."

This woman is my hero. "You don't have to explain to me. I get it. I hope they find him and you can get your alimony."

Nancy tips her head back and laughs, pointing at me. "I like you. Let me know if you want any schnapps—I've got more in my car."

I leave her to make the rounds, playing the doting, grieving wife to the masses. When I finally find Mack and Saint again, Mack is still giggling. My fists clench.

When she spots me, she grabs my arm. "Okay, we've talked to at least a dozen people and no one seems to be out to get you. I think this may be a dead-end."

Behind Mack's bright blonde head, Trevor chats amiably with Officer Rosario. He catches my eye and waves.

"I think you're right," I tell Mack. "I'm pretty sure Nancy isn't my stalker either. She's practically celebrating her husband's disappearance."

"And who could blame her?" Saint takes my hand and nods to the exit. "Let's go."

On our way out, a group of Nancy's friends practically fan themselves as Saint passes. "Any of them wife material?" I tease.

"I'm looking at her." His eyes on me, the sultry note of his voice, make my cheeks burn.

I dart a glance at Mack to make sure she didn't hear that. But her face has gone pale. "What's wrong?"

"I thought . . . I thought I saw someone I recognized." She shakes her head. "Never mind."

During movie night with Mack, she spends half the movie texting. She might be as in love as I am and she hasn't even officially met the guy.

I toss a handful of popcorn in my mouth. "How is your giant, disgusting crush on Zayden Kingsley going?"

She pouts. "Much worse. I found out he's a cat dad. How am I not supposed to fall for my long-distance crush when he has no flaws?"

"I get it. My favorite thing about Saint is how much Cookie likes him."

"Yeah, I bet it's definitely not the hot, wild sex."

"That's certainly high on the list."

Mack sets her phone aside. "Speaking of Saint, how are you two doing after the revelation about your father?"

My blood boils at the mere mention of my father. Of what he did to Saint. What he did to an innocent woman. "Great, actually. You were right—he doesn't resent me for what my family did."

"See? I told you."

He truly is a saint. In every possible way.

Still, now that I know the true extent of my father's depravity, I wonder how much of that depravity exists inside me too. "Do you think you could be capable of murder? In the right circumstances?"

Thankfully, Mack doesn't call me a psycho for asking the question. Instead, she mulls it over for a few seconds. "I'm not entirely sure. But I think maybe. I imagined killing James plenty of times."

He put Mack through hell and back. If anyone deserves to be killed, it's James.

"Now that we know a murderer, maybe you can ask him to take James out." I snort at my own joke.

Mack barks a short laugh. "Please. If anyone gets to murder James, it's me."

Our movie is nearly over when there's a hard thud against the front door. I jump, heart leaping to my throat. "What the hell was that?"

"It sounded like a knock," Mack says slowly. "You want me to answer?"

Jesus. The paranoia has me completely on edge. "No, I've got it."

Through the peephole, the salt and pepper hair, hunched shoulders, and graying eyebrows are so unfamiliar that it takes a second to register the identity of the man waiting on my porch with his hands in his pockets.

My father. Great.

I made it abundantly clear I never wanted to see or speak to him again after he accused Saint of targeting me and ordered him to leave my house. Not to mention I still haven't forgiven him for the whole cheating-on-my-mom-countless-times thing.

I yank the door open. "What the hell are you doing here? I told you I don't want to see you."

His brows are no longer creased in frustration or rage. With his slouched posture and loose skin, he looks every inch the feeble man he's become since the divorce. "I'm leaving town the day after tomorrow. I'd like to have dinner and catch up before I head back, if you want."

I don't have to consider his offer for even a second. "I don't."

He stiffens, but he's not surprised. "Will I be invited to your wedding?"

His words completely baffle me. Saint must've confronted

him after they left my house. He planted the seed of a possible wedding in my father's head. Otherwise, there's no way my father would believe I'd be considering marriage. "Would you even want to attend if I marry him?"

Not that Saint has convinced me to walk down the aisle. He may never convince me. My father ruined the concept of marriage for me, and now he has the audacity to ask for an invitation to my wedding.

Silence falls between us. He can't bring himself to answer.

I nod. "That's what I thought. Have a safe flight home."

Without another word, I shut the door in his face. Somehow, though, when I return to the couch with Mack, the heavy weight on my chest has lifted.

"Was that your father?" Mack asks.

"Yeah. I think I got my closure." The closure Mack told me I needed. I guess she was right.

My best friend gives me a small smile. "Do you feel better?"

"Surprisingly, yes."

I can finally put the past behind me and start a new chapter with Saint. Somehow, I'm glad my father showed up. I'm glad Saint and I discovered the truth about the dark, twisted connection we share. That even though my family shattered his world, I get to be the one to help him put the pieces back together.

We've closed that chapter of our lives. We get to write the rest of our story together.

Now we just need to figure out who the hell is targeting me.

CHAPTER FOURTEEN
SAINT

WHILE BRIAR FINISHES HER WORK DAY, I SIT IN THE library, sending another batch of query letters to the agents listed on the spreadsheet she created.

Immersing myself in the literary world is nearly impossible when my mind is plagued by thoughts of the bastard who thinks he can target my muse. I long to hunt him down and make him suffer ten times the horrors he's inflicted on her. But I also can't leave her on campus alone.

If this madman isn't the groundskeeper or Warren Marshall, then perhaps Briar was right. Perhaps her new stalker is the mysterious blonde in the black BMW.

I text Zayden.

> What can you tell me about the owners of black BMWs in Auburn?

He doesn't respond right away. An email is a welcome distraction from the waiting game until I realize the sender is a literary agent I queried a few days ago.

Dear Mr. Nicholson,
Thank you so much for querying me on DRESSED TO
KILL. Unfortunately, I don't believe I'm the appropriate
agent to represent your work, as the project isn't quite the
right fit for me. I wish you the very best in finding the right
representation for your work.

Rejection is inevitable in this business. Even as a bestselling author of four books, I'm not immune. Sure, more agents and publishers are likely to see a book with my name on it as a money grab than before I was published, but art is subjective and not everyone has acquired a taste for the macabre, darkly romantic Gothic horror novels I pen.

Still, every rejection stings. An ounce of panic zips down my spine at the possibility that this is the end of the road. That I'll only ever publish four books and that the novel I wrote specifically for Briar will never be on her shelf.

My phone buzzes with a text from Zayden.

I'll see what I can find.

The alarm on my phone blares. The sleuthing will have to wait.

I'm outside Briar's classroom when she finally exits after all of her students. She smirks at me but doesn't touch me. Not when there are witnesses.

"Did you send any queries?" she asks while we make our way to the parking lot.

Winter is at last transitioning to spring, students shedding their thick coats and fleece-lined pants for cardigans and leggings. Briar is absolutely radiant in the spring sun.

"A few."

"What's wrong?" Her blue irises examine me, searching for the answers in my features.

"What makes you think something is wrong?"

"Because I know you. Like you know me." She stops to rub at the space between my brows. "You get a crease here." Her finger drifts to the corner of my mouth. "Your lips dip here." She spots her Honda, poking me in the ribs before continuing her trek across the parking lot. "You can't hide from me either."

My chest squeezes. She's the most incredible woman I've ever met. No one has ever loved me like her.

Because I'm certain of it now.

Briar Shea loves me.

"So when are you going to finally admit that you love—"

She gasps.

Her driver's side window has been smashed, broken glass lining the edges, a few pieces glinting on the pavement and more scattered across her driver's seat and floor.

My hands curl into fists. Whoever this monster is, I need to eliminate him. Or her. I can't let this go on a second longer.

"Are you fucking kidding me?" Briar clutches her key in her fist like a dagger. If the assailant were here, I have no doubt she would be stabbing his eye out.

"Stand back. I'll clean this up. I don't want you getting hurt."

"Don't bother." She tugs on my arm and marches me back toward campus. "Come on. We're breaking and entering."

"Where are we breaking into?"

"The security office. They have cameras all over this campus. They must have surveillance footage of the parking lot. If we can hack into it, maybe we can figure out who vandalized my car."

"Can't you ask someone to let you in?"

"They won't let us. Only security personnel are allowed inside."

"Good thing I don't go anywhere without my lock pick."

She rolls her eyes, but a small smile plays on her lips. "For once, I'm actually grateful for your criminal behavior."

"I actually think you were grateful for my criminal behavior the second I broke into your house and licked your pussy."

She elbows me in the ribs, glancing at the students milling around us. "Don't say shit like that where other people can hear you."

I love getting her riled up, even though she should know by now that I would never want to do anything to upset her like getting her fired, even if it meant my life would markedly improve. She is more important than any of my wants or needs. I would gladly stop breathing if she needed my oxygen.

We make our way across the brick campus, trees blooming with new life, nature slowly transitioning from barren and dull to budding and bright. If not for this asshole causing Briar trouble, we could be taking a romantic stroll across a blossoming spring campus. Instead, she's attempting and failing to appear stealthy while beelining for the security office.

As she leads the way into the small faculty building, I tease, "Ah. This place brings back memories."

Briar backhands my arm. "You are the most insufferable man on the planet. We're trying to be incognito here."

"Perhaps you should save the breaking and entering for the professionals, muse."

"It's Professor, Mr. de Haas."

"Excuse me, Professor." I lean down to murmur in her ear. "Shall I be punished for my insolence?"

"As soon as I have the footage I need and I get you alone, you're going to eat those words," she whispers.

I feign a pout. "That's a shame. I was hoping to eat something else."

She ignores me as we reach the campus security office. "I'll stand watch while you pick the lock."

We're alone in the empty hall. I try the knob and it turns. "See, Professor? Leave it to the professionals."

She shoves past me, purposely shouldering my arm as hard as she can. I chuckle and follow her into the dim, cramped room.

"Where the hell do we start?" She shakes both monitors

awake, scanning the live feeds for a camera in the faculty parking lot.

I join her until I spot a feed displaying parked cars and one backing out of its spot. "Here. This is it."

Briar's gaze darts across the monitor. "Let's try to find my car. Should be the shittiest one in the lot, so it shouldn't be hard to spot."

"What are you two doing in here?" A security guard with a buzzcut and a superiority complex glowers at us, arms folded just below the white, all-caps SECURITY label emblazoned across his chest. He's nearly my height, but stocky in a way that tells me he works out for show muscles, not functional strength.

"Oh, Trevor! Thank god."

My lips purse. Thank god? Why the hell would she be thanking a god for sending a security guard to catch us in here?

Briar points at the monitor in front of us. "Somebody smashed the window on my car. We're trying to figure out who it was. Can you help?"

He strides into the room and she smiles, but he turns off the monitors. "You're not allowed to be in here."

Her smile falters. "Trevor, this could be my stalker. If we can get the footage, we'll know who it is."

"And I'm happy to look through the footage for you, but students can't be in here. It's a security protocol." His jaw hardens when his gaze lands on me.

Briar huffs. "Fine. Just please go through it as soon as you can and let me know if you find them. I'm beyond ready to take this bastard down. Did you get anything on the phone number?"

"Not yet. I'll let you know as soon as I hear anything."

"As *soon* as you hear something, and not a second after. This motherfucker needs to get what's coming to them." She flounces out of the room and doesn't notice right away that I'm not following her.

The security guard eyes me and mutters, "Yeah, he does."

"Trevor, is it?"

He straightens but doesn't say anything.

I close the distance between us slowly, resting a hand on his shoulder so anyone passing by may mistake our interaction for friendly. "If anything happens to her because you interfered, you're going to have a much bigger problem on your hands."

He snorts, stepping out of my grasp. "You trying to threaten me, buddy?"

I smirk. "I'm not your buddy, and I'm not trying to threaten you—I am threatening you. If you hinder our efforts to get the evidence needed to keep Briar safe, you won't enjoy the consequences."

His eyes narrow, skin flushing crimson. "I know who you are, pal. Stay the hell away from her."

So she confided in him about me. "I'm not your pal, and I'm not the guy you're looking for. You really think I'd be helping her comb through surveillance footage if I was?"

If not for the dozens of witnesses who could walk in on us at any moment, his hands would be flying for my throat. "I know you're a fucking stalker creep. And I know you've wormed your way into her head." He pokes me square in the chest. "So watch your back."

"Saint," Briar calls, reappearing in the doorway.

If not for her contralto voice rooting me in place, I'd rip this guy's head off.

Without another word, I follow her out the door.

"What was that all about?" she asks while I grab her elbow and pull her down the hallway and out of the building. The spring air now carries an arctic chill.

"You tell me. You certainly seem to know him better than I do."

How has this man been in her life without my knowledge? I know everything about her. Yet Dickhead Trevor somehow slipped through the cracks.

What else has she been hiding from me?

"We're work friends. He was one of the few faculty members who was kind and welcoming to me when I started working here. We'd chat when we saw each other on campus, occasionally have lunch together. I told him about you when you started stalking me, and he offered to help. Apparently, he used to be a cop and still has connections in law enforcement."

Now I really don't like this guy. I had him pinned the second I laid eyes on him. Typical cop with a superiority complex who still thinks he's an authority figure wherever he goes, long after he's turned in his badge. "That explains the hostility. I'm surprised you and Clyde haven't gotten me locked up yet, Bonnie."

Briar rolls her eyes. "We're not Bonnie and Clyde or Velma and Daphne or Thelma and Louise or any other notorious duo you can think of. He's just trying to be a good friend. He knows you've been stalking me, so it's not exactly surprising that he thinks you're the one behind all of this."

"Yes, that certainly would make someone the primary suspect to an ex-cop."

"Excuse me for trying to protect my own ass."

"As long as you're done with him now, I won't kill him."

She tugs me to a stop sharply. "Saint, don't hurt him. He's my friend, and he's just trying to look out for me. And for your own good, I'm telling you—don't go after Trevor. If he has the connections he says he does, you won't get away with it this time."

As much as I loathe to admit it, she has a point. Trevor would be a far more difficult target to eliminate discreetly than Austin Emmons or Professor Molester. Trevor likely already has experience with men like me and he's still standing.

"Just stay away from him."

She smiles sweetly, batting her lashes, and I brace myself for a sarcastic quip. "Don't worry. I'll stay away right after I deliver his baby."

Briar's mother is back in town, and this time, Briar is the one who invites me to join them for dinner.

I buy two bouquets on my way to the restaurant, unable to fight the delighted grin.

She wouldn't be inviting me to dinner with her mother if our relationship wasn't growing more serious. Wedding bells practically echo in my ears, visions of kneeling when they bring out dessert flashing through my mind.

Fighting the urge to spontaneously propose tonight will be nearly impossible, but I've already determined how I'll be proposing to her: in the dedication of my next book. The book I was only able to write because I met her. My muse.

Besides, the last thing Briar needs on her plate right now is wedding planning. First, we need to eliminate the asshole harassing her. Once that's handled and she finishes out the semester, she can move in with me, and I'll propose as soon as my next book is published, when all she'll have on her plate is wedding planning and writing and reading to her heart's content.

The restaurant is upscale, a splurge to celebrate her promotion. I pay with my card before the host leads me to our table, where Briar and Cecilia are already seated. I hand a bouquet to each of them before taking the seat beside my muse.

Cecilia's face lights up. "Oh, Saint! What a sweet gesture. Thank you!"

"It's my pleasure." I plant a kiss on Briar's cheek, and if possible, Cecilia's smile widens.

Briar barely registers my existence, however. Engrossed in her phone, the bouquet of flowers neglected on the table in front of her.

"Aren't the flowers so beautiful?" Cecilia prompts.

Briar's gaze lifts, finally noticing the bouquet. "Oh. Yes, that was very sweet. Thank you." She offers me a small smile.

The evening continues like this while we order appetizers and entrees, Cecilia asking me about my books and how the new one is coming along while I indulge her, inquiring about her work—retired early—and her hobbies—bridge and book club—and her favorite recipes, each relayed to me in great detail. All the while, Briar remains disengaged from the conversation, eyes glued to her phone. In the rare moments that she turns off her screen, her attention remains elsewhere.

She needs a reminder that when she and I are together, nothing else matters. Nothing else exists.

When her mother finishes recounting a peanut butter brittle recipe, she shifts her attention to her daughter. "Is everything all right, dear?"

Briar continues tuning us out as she has all evening.

"Briar," Cecilia prompts, more insistent now.

My muse manages to drag her gaze up from her screen, open to a text thread with an unsaved number. The scumbag who's been harassing her. I clench my jaw, hands curling into fists under the table.

Her new stalker is the one who has ensnared her attention. This should be a celebratory night. Her promotion a new milestone in her life, in our relationship. Instead, she's fixating on someone else.

I'm sick of allowing this bastard to come between us. And I won't rest until I hunt them down and bury them six feet under, where they belong.

"Is something wrong, sweetheart?" Cecilia implores. "Is it work?"

Briar huffs, shoving her phone away. "No, Mom, it's not work." She pokes at her lasagna with complete disinterest.

"Well, then I'm not sure what's so important that you need to ignore your mother and boyfriend all evening."

Briar stiffens, but I'm grateful when she doesn't correct her mother about the nature of our relationship. "I just have a lot going on, all right?"

Cecilia leans closer, lowering her voice and failing to disguise the hurt. "I just don't understand what's gotten into you lately. We've always been so close, but you've been shutting me out and keeping secrets."

Briar jumps up from her seat, throwing her napkin onto the table. "I'm going to use the restroom."

As soon as my muse is out of sight, Cecilia drops her gaze back to her plate. "I am so sorry about that, Saint. I expected this to be a nice evening."

"Briar has a lot on her plate. I'm sure she'll be back to her old self once she settles into this new job."

Cecilia manages a small smile. "Thank you. But I know my daughter. There's something else going on with her that she's not telling us. Briar has always been very independent. She refuses to accept help from anyone, and when she's facing a challenge, she keeps it to herself because she doesn't want to burden anyone else. Especially me. She knows as her mother that her burdens are my burdens, and ever since her father's indiscretion, she's taken up the role of my protector, even though the roles should be reversed."

I almost laugh. I'm well aware of Briar's reluctance to accept help or show vulnerability. "As a more permanent fixture in Briar's life now, I'll happily protect you both."

Cecilia squeezes my hand. "I'm very happy my daughter has you."

"And I'm delighted and humbled every day to have found her."

Except right now, Briar is pulling away from me too. If she wants to spare her mother her burdens, I won't stop her. But she should know better than to try to conceal her worries from me. I live to protect her, to keep her safe, and she's not doing either of us any favors by shutting me out.

"I'll go check on her. Would you mind ordering dessert? I've got my eye on that chocolate peanut butter pie."

Cecilia happily agrees, and I head for the ladies' room,

knocking and announcing my arrival before pushing the door open.

Fortunately, all of the stalls are empty except one. As soon as I reach the door, Briar swings it open and pulls me in.

Her cheeks are tear-stained, and my blood boils knowing that bastard made her cry. I will prolong his torment until he's begging me to put him out of his misery.

"Your mother and I are worried about you."

She rolls her eyes. "Please don't tell me you're ganging up on me with my mother."

"No one is ganging up on you. We're on your side."

She shakes her head. "Tonight was a bad idea. I don't know why I thought I would be in the mood to celebrate right now."

"Because there will always be bad things happening alongside the good. So you need to celebrate the good when you can."

"God, you sound like a pretentious writer."

I smirk. "You've got me pegged."

She lifts a taunting brow. "Is that your kink?"

I push her up against the stall wall. "Not in the slightest."

"Oh, you wouldn't let me try it? What if it's just a little dildo? Six inches, tops."

I kiss her to shut her up. "We better get back to your mother. She's ordering pie."

"Then I'd estimate we have at least ten minutes."

"You want to do this here? Now?" I will never decline her if she says she wants me, even on my deathbed, but she was crying two minutes ago.

Her hands unfasten my belt buckle hastily. "Yes. I need a distraction."

My spine stiffens. "Is that all I am to you? A momentary distraction from everything you wish to forget?"

She straightens, lifting her chin to meet my gaze with a surprising fierceness in those bright blue eyes. "Not at all. You mean much more to me than that."

My black heart grows three sizes, and I squeeze her chin. "Then don't refer to fucking me as a distraction again."

"I won't," she promises, rubbing at my erection before reaching a hand into my pants and stroking my cock.

My fingers find their way up her dress and into her panties, making her breath hitch when I find her clit and press down.

"I want you to fuck me hard and fast," she murmurs, spinning to face the stall wall and planting her hands by her shoulders.

No preamble then. Just railing her in a public restroom stall. Fucking away the stress.

I shove her panties to the side and sheath my cock inside her. She hisses through her teeth but manages to swallow down her cries. Her tight walls around my shaft feel fucking euphoric.

"You're my bad fucking girl."

She beams at me over her shoulder. "So punish me for how bad I've been."

I slam into her, making her gasp and regret those words. Her pussy walls tighten around my cock, and my eyes roll. Fuck, she's incredible.

I wedge a hand between her and the stall, rubbing at her clit as her ass bounces with every thrust. The stall walls rattle around us as I attempt to bite down my own groans of pleasure.

Her pussy starts to clench around my cock and my balls tighten just as the restroom door creaks open. We freeze, waiting for Briar's mother to call out her name until we hear an unfamiliar voice. "What's going on in there?"

"Fuck off!" Briar yells, rocking back into me. I can't help the involuntary groan that escapes.

The woman clucks in disgust. "You should be ashamed of yourselves!"

Briar keeps rocking back into me, no longer suppressing her moans of ecstasy.

The woman's heels click out of the room and she slams the door behind her.

With one final jerk back against my cock, Briar loses herself, hands slipping down the stall wall and moaning so loud, I clap a hand over her mouth before the whole restaurant knows exactly what we're doing in here.

As she unravels in front of me, my own orgasm barrels through me, cock jumping inside her tight pussy as ropes of cum shoot out and fill her. I shudder against her, pleasure coursing through my veins.

When I can finally bring myself to pull out, we're both panting.

"Wow. So that's how you fuck your girlfriend, huh?"

So she was listening to our dinner conversation. At least parts of it. "No. You've been my wife since I laid eyes on you."

She snorts. "I want a ring before you start calling me your wife."

"You'll get whatever ring you want. But I'm calling you my wife now."

"Until death do us part?" She's teasing, sarcasm dripping from her lips as she maintains the ridiculous notion that she'll never marry me, but she'll soon learn that I mean exactly what I say.

"No. Even when death comes for me, I'm crawling from my grave to find you in the afterlife."

She can't help the smile that tugs at her lips. "I've always wanted a man who would crawl to me."

CHAPTER FIFTEEN
BRIAR

A HARD KNOCK ON MY FRONT DOOR MAKES ME FLINCH AND sends Cookie running to hide.

Through the peephole, a scowling blonde in a ponytail is waiting on my porch. A black BMW in my driveway.

My heart stops.

The blonde in the BMW who's been following me. She isn't lurking in the shadows anymore—she's showing up at my front door in broad daylight.

She isn't wearing a uniform, but don't private investigators opt for casual clothes to blend in?

I could ignore her. I *should* ignore her. But I want to end this shit.

Impossibly, her scowl deepens when I yank the door open. "Can I help you?"

"I'm sure you can." Her husky voice is vaguely familiar.

She strides for the open door before I jump out and slam it shut behind me. "You're not coming into my house."

Her eyes narrow. "Have something to hide?"

"No, I just have a rule about not inviting crazy stalkers to waltz through my front door. You'll have to break in like the rest of them."

Her lips thin, but she doesn't deny the accusation. "What aren't you telling the police about the night my brother died?"

The pieces click into place. *April.*

This is Austin's sister. The woman on the phone who delivered the news about Austin's death. Who was obviously suspicious of me when I offered to return her brother's watch.

My heart hammers harder, panic mixing with the relief. April is the one who's been stalking me. Ever since that phone call, she's been following me, trying to find proof that her brother's overdose wasn't accidental and I'm the one responsible. She followed me to campus, to Nicholson Manor, and now she's located my address.

I expected that Saint and I would spend the next weeks or even months tracking her down. Now she's standing on my front porch, willingly revealing her identity to me.

"I don't know anything I haven't told the police," I lie. "Austin and I met up for tacos that night, we walked back to my house, we kissed, and he left. That's it. I didn't even know he used drugs."

"He didn't," April snaps. "He'd been clean for months. Then he spends one night with you, and suddenly he dies of an overdose? Are you trying to tell me that's some sort of coincidence?"

I clench my teeth at the implication. I'm sure Austin led his sister to believe he was clean, even if that was far from the truth. Regardless, I'm not to blame for his death, and I'm sick of being accused of shit I didn't do. "Look, I'm sorry for your loss. But I didn't have anything to do with your brother turning up dead."

She shakes her head in disgust, ponytail swaying. "I should've known you were shady when you brought up his watch. Who gives a shit about a watch when someone is dead?"

"Your brother is the one who was shady. I'm telling you I didn't do anything or give anything to him."

"I don't believe you."

She can join the club with Officer Smith.

"Believe what you want. But that's the truth." I point to her

BMW in my driveway. "Now get off my property before I call the cops."

Her eyes narrow on me like she wants to rip my hair from my scalp or claw out my eyes. I should've brought a knife or a pan or *something* to defend myself with. Hell, I don't even have my car keys to stab her in the eye if she tries to kill me with her bare hands. She's slender, but tall and lithe. Probably a runner. Probably a gym rat with visible biceps beneath the sweater.

She's a crazed stalker who wants me to pay for her brother's death. She could attack me right now. Kill me.

But she retreats a step.

"Stop stalking me," I demand, hating the way my voice wobbles.

"I don't know what you're talking about." She squeezes the wooden porch railing so hard, I brace for it to splinter. "But you're not getting away with this forever, Briar. I don't care how long it takes—I'll get justice for my brother."

I wait until her black BMW disappears down the road before calling Saint. We finally have the answer we've been searching for—my mysterious stalker's identity.

"Muse?"

"I know who's stalking me."

Trevor calls out to me as I rush to my office before my first class of the day. My smile is bright, my steps lighter now that I know April is the one behind everything and I can tell Trevor the news.

But my stomach twists when I spot the person at his side. A short man with a beard and a police uniform.

Trevor waves me over, and I try to slow my breathing and my racing heart.

"Briar!" He flashes me a warm smile. "This is my buddy, Dan. He's agreed to take your statement about your stalker."

I push down the unease that bubbles to the surface. So far, the police haven't exactly been receptive to anything I've said.

"We really encourage you to make an official report," Dan says. "You can come down to the station anytime and personally request me to take your statement."

"I think your department is done listening to me." I offer him a sickly sweet smile. "In fact, I don't think any of you have been listening to me from the beginning."

Dan frowns sympathetically. "I understand you've recently been connected to two unfortunate incidents. But if you're being stalked, it's possible there could be a connection. By reporting what you're experiencing, you could potentially help us solve Dr. Charles Barrett's disappearance."

I glance at Trevor, who nods encouragingly. "You can tell him, Briar. He's here to listen."

Trevor's trying to be a good friend, and Dan is likely his buddy down at the station who's been helping us with the investigation so far. Maybe he doesn't share Smith's and Rosario's suspicions of me.

"Actually," I admit, taking a deep breath, "I am pretty sure I've identified my stalker."

Trevor brightens while Dan pulls out a notepad. "Really? Who would that be?"

"Her name is April Emmons."

Skepticism narrows Trevor's gaze. He's still convinced that Saint is behind all of this. Like it's not possible for me to have two stalkers.

"She's Austin's sister," I explain. "I guess she somehow thinks I'm involved in Austin's death, so she's been following me."

I relay all of the information to Dan—April following me to campus, watching me through a window, breaking in and chasing me through the house, the repeated silent phone calls, the creepy texts, destroying my car window, showing up at my house demanding to know more about the night Austin died.

Dan scribbles it all down, nodding. The first time a police

officer has truly listened and taken me seriously. "Thank you, Briar. If you want to come down to the station sometime, we'll make an official report."

"Thank you. That would be great." Maybe I'll actually get this crazy girl off my back. For the first time in a while, hope fills my chest. This is almost over.

Once Officer Dan shakes Trevor's hand and heads back to the parking lot, I smile at my friend. "Thanks for that. It felt good to have someone in law enforcement actually take me seriously for once."

"You really should follow up on that report," he encourages before chewing on his lip. "But Briar . . ."

"What?"

"Are you sure this April chick is actually stalking you?"

I narrow my eyes. "I know she's been following me. I've seen her car. It was the same black BMW in my driveway when she showed up at my house."

"Yeah, but are you sure she's responsible for everything else? The texts, the calls? How would she have even gotten your number?" he asks. "You already know your student has it."

My hands ball into fists. "Oh my god. This is still about Saint? Yes, he was stalking me before, okay? But he's not behind any of that. He didn't stalk me to scare me or hurt me. And that's what this person is doing. That's what *April* has been doing."

I appreciate everything Trevor has done to help me. But he has this completely wrong. Saint wouldn't terrorize me like this.

He loves me.

And I . . . I may love him too.

Trevor sighs and shakes his head. "I hope you're right, Briar," he says. "I really hope he doesn't hurt you."

CHAPTER SIXTEEN
SAINT

APRIL EMMONS IS NO STALKER. SHE'S A TWENTY-TWO-YEAR-old law school student, now the singular heir to her father's firm.

Zayden's voice drones in my ear. "She should be ordering an iced lavender latte."

From the sidewalk, my gaze zeros in on the blonde in a ponytail holding a latte, a laptop bag slung over her opposite shoulder as she pushes her way out of the coffee shop.

"Your skills are disturbing," I inform him. Even from another country, Zayden is capable of accessing an American's credit card transactions and daily routine.

"And yet you always seem to be in need of them. Do you have eyes on her?"

"I do. I'll be in touch." I end the call and tuck my phone in my pocket.

April hesitates when I approach her, but she relaxes when I flash her a smile. "Mind if I bother you a moment?"

"Is it bothering if I welcome it?" she simpers, shielding her gaze against the bright sun.

I can't force the smile to stay glued to my face. No woman should believe I want anything from her. My muse is everything I could want or desire. April is of no use to me other than the information she can provide. "I understand that you believe the last person to see your brother, Austin, alive could be the one responsible for his death."

April's demeanor shifts from flirtatious interest to irritated skepticism. "I might. Who's asking?"

"I'm a private investigator looking into the case."

Her eyes narrow. "My family hasn't hired any private investigators."

"Why would they when you seem so keen on becoming one yourself?" I challenge. She opens her mouth to tell me off, but I continue. "I've been hired by Dr. Charles Barrett's family. If this woman is responsible for Austin's death, as you presume, she could be connected to Dr. Barrett's disappearance as well."

April glances around us for prying eyes or eavesdropping ears before she steps closer and lowers her voice. "Her name is Briar Shea. She works at the Auburn Institute of Fine Arts, and she claims she didn't know Austin before that night. Yet he meets her and conveniently shows up dead the next morning?" Her lips form a thin line. "And somehow the police still haven't made an arrest."

"As a law student, you should know there's insufficient evidence."

She tilts her head. "You know I'm a law student. I thought you were investigating Briar Shea, not me."

"I learn everything I can about all parties involved. When there are no clear answers, everyone is a suspect."

"Oh, so I killed my brother now?" She rolls her eyes and retreats.

"Not that I can tell. Though I am wondering how you managed to track down Briar's address. You're the law student— is that legal?"

"You claim to be a PI. Shouldn't you know?" She shrugs. "I'll do what I need to do to get justice for my brother."

"Someone on the inside gave you the information." I close the distance between us, towering over her now. "Who was it?"

Fear colors her features before she turns on her heel, striding down the sidewalk. "We're done here."

I fall into step beside her. I'm this close to uncovering the information I need to keep my muse safe. I won't let April leave until she reveals it. "Who's the officer you had to blow for information?"

Her eyes flash before they narrow. I was bluffing, but it worked. "Forget it," she snaps.

"Do you really want an officer on the force who bribes women into sex for confidential information?" I grab her arm, pulling her to a stop. "You really think Austin would want that?"

April hesitates, gaze falling to the ground as tears glisten at the memory of her brother. Little does she know, her hero big brother probably sold women to that same corrupt cop.

But I'll allow her to keep that untainted memory of her brother if she gives me the information I need.

"He said his name is Trevor."

When I cross the threshold into Briar's bedroom, she's already stretched out across her bed in red lingerie, waiting for me.

My god, she's heavenly. The bra prominently displays her breasts, pushing them up for my enjoyment, a large bow between them with tail ends that extend down to her navel like she's a present begging to be unwrapped. Her lace thong is little more than a *V*, the sheer fabric hardly accomplished in hiding her pussy from me.

If I wrote a thousand autobiographies with a thousand different predictions of how my life would turn out, I never could've written a twist where I get this lucky.

I grin. "You knew I was coming here. Are you stalking me, sinner?"

"I like when you call me sinner." Briar beams. "And I wanted to surprise you."

"Surprise me as often as you like."

Briar crawls across the mattress to me and my cock twitches, but I need her to know what I've discovered.

"April isn't your stalker."

Her blue eyes harden. "I don't want to talk about any of that right now."

"We need to," I tell her. "She—"

"Stop, Saint. None of that matters right now. Nothing else exists when we're like this, remember? When it's just the two of us. All of that can wait."

I can't argue with her. When she's in front of me, the rest of the world grows quiet. Everything I've learned about April and Trevor can wait.

Tomorrow, I'll verify April's story that Trevor was impersonating a police officer and feeding her Briar's information.

My muse kneels at the edge of the bed and takes my hands in hers. Eyes softening and imploring. "You would never hurt me. Right?"

If she's asking, that means she's still uncertain. Even after everything—after I've played out her wildest fantasies, after she's let me inside her, after I've killed for her—she still doesn't fully trust me. The ache settles deep in my chest. "Never."

"Good," she whispers against my mouth. "I want to do every position you've ever fantasized about having me in."

My hand travels down to her ass to cup a cheek. "Every position?"

Lust burns fiery in her blue eyes. "Yes."

I'm rock-hard now. "I don't care if I need to convince you every day for the rest of our lives that I love you. I will do so with my dying breath."

She melts in my grasp like butter, allowing me to tip her head back as I sweep her into a passionate kiss.

"You're my everything, Briar. Without you, I am nothing."

She flashes a small smirk. "I get it. You're a writer."

I push her down onto the bed, landing on her, our lips

brushing together. This time already feels more intimate than all the others that came before it.

"I'm tired of fucking you with your clothes on." Her hands unfasten the buttons on my shirt.

I smirk. "I can't help it that you're always in such a rush to get my cock inside you."

"Well, tonight we're taking our time."

I drag my fingers through her mahogany hair, attempting to memorize every inch of her perfect face. The round, bright cerulean eyes with the dark lashes and pale purple bags underneath from all her sleepless nights. The small forehead, mostly hidden by a full hairline. The round cheeks that descend to a slightly pointed chin. The nose that perks up at the tip. The dark, arched brows that betray her every emotion. The mole on her jawline that distinguishes her from all of the other beautiful women with flawless skin. The pouty pink lips, always turned up in a taunting smirk or pursed in disapproval. Except in the rare moments they curl up to display her teeth in a genuine smile. Or when her eyes flutter shut and her mouth falls open in a joyous laugh. Both so rare that whenever she blesses you with them, you know you've earned them.

She never lets anyone in. Except when she finally does. And then you never want her to let you go.

Briar tugs my shirt off, cold hands traveling over my shoulders, stopping to squeeze my biceps with a smile. "Have I ever told you how sexy you are?"

"Your eyes tell me every time you see me."

"My eyes need to shut the fuck up."

I chuckle. "They're very chatty. They cannot keep a secret."

She giggles, and I can't decide which sound I prefer—her laughter or her ecstasy.

Briar continues helping me undress until I'm fully naked in front of her. Her hands are warmer now, skimming over my pecs down to the hard ridges of my abs before she drags a nail across my pelvic bone. I shudder as my cock twitches.

"I will never not be in awe of this," she whispers.

"I will never not be in awe of you."

Her reaction to my words is unexpected. Her brows pull together, frown tugging down the corners of her mouth. "Why me?"

"Why you what?"

"Why did you choose me?"

I skim a finger down her cheek, soft and delicate. Nothing at all like the fiery, spitfire woman she is. But exactly like the heart she conceals. "Because you're my muse. We were meant for each other."

The scowl still doesn't leave her lips. "I guess I just don't understand that. Everything I write is out of spite. My muses are all the people I've ever hated."

I can't help but laugh. Of course they are. "Before I met you, I only knew you as the faceless user online declaring herself my biggest fan in her book reviews." She blushes, even now. "I wrote all my books for you, even before I met you. I knew, deep in my soul, that somehow, my words would find you. Find that one person in the universe who would read them and understand. I'd read your reviews on my darkest days and remember why I did this. Why I kept toiling away on books that seemed to fade into obscurity as soon as they entered the literary world. Why I kept pouring all my blood, sweat, and tears into books that no one would read. Except you. And you were enough. You've always been enough, Briar."

She swipes at a tear that escapes her misty eyes.

"I kept writing because of you. I wrote *This Book Will Haunt You* because I thought you'd love it. I included all of the elements of my previous books that you said you loved most. And that book became my bestseller. It made my previous books bestsellers. And then, when I thought I was a broken writer, when I lamented that I'd never be able to write another word again, there you were. The light in my darkness once more. I finally met my biggest fan in person and listening to you gush about my words, watching the excitement light up your eyes, something clicked in my mind. The dam broke. The words flowed again. All because of you. And I knew the second I spoke to you, the moment our eyes connected, that everything has been because of you. Everything that's happened, every step I've taken, has been a journey to find you. The other half of my soul. The missing piece to my puzzle that I've been searching for my entire life. I know I've fallen faster and harder than you have. You may not love me yet. Or, if you do, you may not be willing to admit it. But I promise you, I will gladly devote every day of my life to proving my worth to you. And even if I don't hear those three words from your lips until I'm on my deathbed, I will die a happy man."

Silence falls between us for a few moments, Briar letting my words sink in while she tries to come up with her own. She wipes uselessly at a tear only for the next to follow. "I don't deserve you."

And even though they're not the three words I want to hear, they're enough to make my chest squeeze with the hope that someday I will. "You deserve everything I can give you and more."

She pulls me down to kiss her, and I sweep my tongue into her mouth, luxuriating in her sweet taste and the moan rising from her throat.

There is only one other woman—one other person—in this world I would've died for, but Briar is the only one left. I will do anything to keep her safe, to keep her in my arms for as long as I can. Anything.

My finger hooks in the lace bra pushing up her gorgeous tits. "Please tell me you bought this for me."

"Of course not. Can't you tell how old it is?"

A smile plays on my lips as my hand drifts to the band. "And yet, you still haven't removed the tag."

She rips the tag off, tossing it aside. "Just because I haven't worn it yet doesn't mean I bought it recently. Certainly not for you."

"Right. You wouldn't do anything for me."

Her smile slips away now, a rare moment of vulnerability crossing her face. "I would do a lot for you," she whispers.

Fuck. My heart stutters. I wind a strand of her soft hair around my finger, leaning in to brush my lips against hers. Fingers drifting down to draw across her collarbones. Her throat. "Would you kill for me, muse?"

Would she do all that I've already proven I'm willing to do for her?

Her chest rises and falls faster, breaths turning shallow. "If you needed me to . . . yes."

My eyes fall shut. Briar loves me. Even if she can't bring herself to say it out loud, her answer tells me all I need to know about her true feelings for me.

"As long as they're human," she adds. "If you ask me to kill a cat, you can fuck right off."

"Of course they would be human. I'm not a monster." I slip the knot on her bra free, the cups falling to the side and exposing her plump breasts to me. I cradle them both, admiring how heavy they weigh on my palms before pushing them together. "I want to shove my cock between these."

"I did say we can do every position you want," she grumbles.

I grin like a teenager about to fuck a woman for the first time. "And I do hope you keep your promises."

My lips wrap around her nipple before she can say another word. She gasps and arches into my mouth, forcing me to take her deeper. She's always hungry for me. For more. Insatiable.

Briar tugs at my hair, pain lancing through my scalp, and I savor the way it anchors me to her, to this moment. I grind my erection against her thigh, already dry-humping her from how eager I am to slip inside her.

Her nipple pops out of my mouth, her tit wobbling as I

move to the other. She cries out as I suck her peaked nipple hard enough to bruise.

"I want you covered in bruises and cum when I'm finished with you. Reminders of everything I'm going to do to you tonight. Of everything I can make you feel. Of the ecstasy only I can give you."

She whimpers, and her voice comes out in a small whisper, "Please."

Rarely does she freely plea for anything. "I do love hearing you beg, muse."

Briar shudders at my breath caressing the shell of her ear. I tug her lobe between my teeth, enjoying the way she writhes beneath me.

"Don't get used to it."

God, she never fails to make me smile. "A happier man does not exist on this planet when I'm with you."

She grins, sucking on my neck and eliciting a low groan from my throat before I trail kisses down her body. "Neither does a happier woman."

I squeeze her close before looping a finger through her thong. "I want to rip through this. But I also want to see it on you again."

"Too bad this is the one and only time I'll be feeling generous."

"You'll be feeling very generous by the time I'm through with you."

She gasps when I abruptly yank her thong down her legs, spreading her wide and admiring. I rub her clit softly while keeping my gaze trained on her face. Her eyes flutter shut as her breathing hitches, back arching slightly off the mattress.

I lean down to swallow her moans, trailing kisses along her jawline and down her neck to her collarbone, unable to get enough of her. Needing my mouth and hands on every inch.

My mouth travels back down to her breast, taking in her nipple. I alternate between sucking and swirling my tongue around the sensitive spot, luxuriating in her until she finally lets out a whimper and pushes my head away. A hickey blooms in my wake, and I fully intend to abuse the other the same way.

"You're driving me crazy," she grinds out.

"You're well past crazy, my little sinner."

She shoves my head down to where she aches for me. I love that she believes she's the one in control, even though it's my tongue coaxing every moan and gasp and shudder from her body.

I kiss down to her mound, trailing a path around her pussy and to her thighs. Her muscles are tight, tension already strung through every limb as she aches for release.

"Don't torment me again."

I splay a hand across her chest, gliding down over her smooth, soft skin. "This body of yours belongs to me. I will do with it as I wish, when I wish."

She huffs through her nose like a bull. "You are the most aggravating man I've ever met."

"I think you mean arousing."

Before she can argue, I bury my head between her legs.

My mouth on her pussy is nearly as delightful as my cock inside it. A single command from my tongue has her whole body writhing. Her sweet taste floods my tongue when I stroke up to that bundle of nerves, making the pleasure mount in her limbs until I press tender kisses to her clit and lips.

She whimpers in frustration, tugging at my hair to get my tongue back on her pussy. But I continue the torment with my kisses, not giving her the satisfaction she seeks. Yet.

Just as I will need to be patient to earn her trust, her heart, she'll need to be patient to earn her orgasm.

My tongue swirls gently around her clit, circling the sensitive nub but never making direct contact. Her hands ball into fists, and she slams them down onto the mattress, emitting a wild screech of frustration. I can't help but chuckle between her legs.

"It's not funny!" she rages. "Wait until I get my mouth on you and make you regret this."

"Wonderful," I mutter, my breath hitting her swollen clit. "Edging is my kink."

"You son of a—"

The insult dies in her throat when I wrap my lips around her clit and suck.

"Agh!" she cries out, back arching. Her pussy pushes against my mouth. I grip her ass, pulling her deeper into my mouth as I suck her clit as hard as I sucked her bruised nipples.

"Fuck! Don't stop. *Please.*"

At the plea from her lips, I oblige her, my mouth continuing its assault on her pretty little pussy.

Her wetness drips out and my finger slips inside. She moans when I curl it to hit that sweet spot.

I thrust my finger slowly in and out of her as she claws at my hair, making my eyes sting. She could slice me open, shoot me, and I still wouldn't stop until I made her come. "Are you going to come on my finger, muse?"

"Yes." She's breathless now, on the brink of overwhelming pleasure.

My finger thrusts fast and hard as I continue sucking her clit, the swollen nub throbbing in my mouth as I bring her to orgasm, hard and fast, not letting her escape it even if she tried.

"Fuck! Saint!" Her nails claw at the sheet, ripping it up from the mattress. Her thighs shake around my head as the rest of her body writhes, torn between savoring the pleasure my mouth is giving her and escaping the overwhelming ecstasy of it.

I don't relieve her of the hard, punishing pressure from my mouth or the finger slamming inside her until her pussy stops pulsing. I drop her sensitive, aching clit from my mouth and lap at it gently, slowing the thrust of my finger to come down from the orgasm with her.

"Feeling generous yet?"

She rolls her eyes, even as she nudges my shoulder to push

me onto my back. I grin and prop my head on my arm when she kneels between my legs. "*This* is the one and only time I'll be generous," she corrects.

"Better make it unforgettable then."

Her sharp blue eyes flash to mine. "It will be."

I swallow. My god, this woman.

Briar uses both hands to explore my collarbones, pecs, and abdomen. No one has ever admired my physique like she has. Like someone who's never seen art marveling at a statue hewn from gold.

When she's finished, she drags a nail between my hip bones. I am putty in her hands, cock nearly so hard it hurts as a bead of precum rises to the surface.

"That's so cute," she purrs. "Already about to come and I haven't even gotten my mouth on you yet."

"Let me worship that wicked tongue," I pant. Her hands have dissolved me to a pleading, horny teenage boy entirely too quickly.

She grins. "I do love hearing you beg."

Her head drops down, but instead of taking my throbbing cock in her mouth, she trails delicate kisses from one hip to the other, gradually descending until she's circling the base of my cock, lips never brushing against my aching shaft.

I fist my hands in her hair. "Jesus Christ, Briar."

She clucks her tongue. "So impatient."

"I've created a monster."

"Not created," she corrects. "Awoken."

I grin, but it slips away the second her palm cups my balls. I hiss through my teeth, thrusting deeper into her hand. "Are you going to come for me?" she taunts.

"For you. In you. On you."

"Someone's a little *cocky*." Briar gently flicks the tip of my dick and I nearly shout.

Fuck, if this is anything like the torture I put her through, I'm amazed she didn't beg for mercy.

"You think I'm going to allow you to come in *and* on me?"

"I know I'm going to."

"I don't know . . ." She trails a nail from my tip down the length of my shaft, over the throbbing vein until she reaches my balls. "I think a few quick pumps of my hand will have you coming all over your own stomach. Nowhere near me."

I smirk. "Who said anything about only coming once?"

"I don't think you'll have any more cum to give after this one." She cups my balls again, squeezing the tip of my cock with her other hand.

I grit my teeth, attempting to keep the load from shooting out. "I'll always have enough to fill that pretty throat and tight little cunt."

She shrugs. "We'll see about that."

Finally, her head dips down, sucking the tip of my cock into her mouth. She swirls her tongue around it, making my cock twitch when her tongue strokes the underside.

"Shit," I grind out.

"Mmm." The sound reverberates down my shaft to my tight balls.

She wraps her hand around my shaft, stroking down slowly until she reaches the base and squeezes my balls with the other hand.

Damn it. She plays my body like an instrument too. A violin strung too tight, and the next pluck of her fingers will make all my strings snap.

"You're trying so hard not to come, aren't you?" she teases.

I am this close to fisting her hair and forcing her mouth down the length of my cock, but I enjoy her playing too much to stop her. "I could go for an hour like this."

Briar lifts a brow at the challenge, not dropping my cock from her mouth. She swallows my hard length almost to her hand wrapped around the middle before gagging slightly and dragging her mouth back up. Her hand squeezing my cock moves up to the tip before gliding back down, lubricating every inch with her saliva. Pleasure builds to an excruciating point.

"You can come," she coos. "I won't be disappointed."

Now she'll have to deep-throat my cock if she wants a single drop of my cum.

Her mouth bobs up and down the top of my dick while her hand strokes the inches she can't swallow, her other hand still playing with my balls. Watching her enjoy me is almost too much to bear. "Gag on it."

She ignores me, continuing to swallow down only as much as she can comfortably handle. When her mouth is about to ascend again, I thrust my hips up.

A loud, sharp groan escapes my lips at the same time her gag fills my ears. Her hands drop my shaft and balls as she clutches at my thighs. But I don't care when I thread my fingers around the back of her scalp to keep her head in place while I fuck her throat.

Briar gurgles around my cock, nails drawing blood from my thighs as my cock continues slamming into the back of her throat, pleasure pulsing through every vein until I can't hold back anymore, and my cock explodes, cum pouring into her throat.

She gags, tears spilling down her cheeks as she struggles to swallow it all with no other choice.

"That's so fucking sexy," I purr. "Swallow every drop, sinner."

She finally stops gurgling and heaving when the last drop of cum slides down her throat, and I pull my cock from her lips.

Droplets of blood stain my thighs from where her nails broke the skin. When she notices, she narrows her eyes. "I don't feel bad. You deserve that."

"I will happily let you make me bleed if it means I can make you swallow."

Briar purses her lips, not at all thrilled with my compromise yet happily straddling my half-hard cock. "That was the extent of my generosity."

My hand slips around to her ass, pinching the flesh there. "I seem to remember a promise to indulge my every whim in any position."

"I never said your every whim." She rolls her eyes. "But I suppose I did agree to any position."

"Excellent." I flip her onto her back, nudging her legs apart and rubbing the tip of my cock against her clit until her thighs are trembling again and her whimpers make blood pound through my shaft.

I move up her body, shoving her tits together. She groans.

"You said any position I desire," I remind her.

"Yeah, but a titty fuck?"

"With tits this extraordinary, how can I possibly resist?"

She rolls her eyes, but a smile sneaks across her lips at the praise. She will never admit out loud how much she craves my words of affirmation. How much she worships my tongue, whether it's forming words of adoration or licking her pussy.

My cock is still slick with the saliva from her mouth when I shove it between her glorious tits, the tip hitting her lips. She doesn't part them, and I draw back, dragging my cock back down until I thrust forward, harder this time.

Her mouth opens involuntarily for me, my cock driving past her lips and dragging along her tongue. I groan, practically salivating at the sight of her beneath me, jaw coming unhinged and blue eyes round as I fuck her tits and mouth. Every time I thrust my tip past her lips, my cock drags her saliva back with me, lubricating the skin between her breasts and making me hungry for more. Her throat, her pussy, her ass. I want her in every way imaginable.

I drop her breasts and move back down her body, finger curling against her still-sensitive clit. Her breath catches.

"I'm going to fuck your pussy now, muse." Her body relaxes beneath my touch until I add, "And then wherever else I choose."

"What—"

But the words are ripped from her throat when I drive my cock into her pussy.

She cries out, back arching as she jerks violently at the sudden intrusion. "*Fuck!*"

"I already came in you. Shall I come on you next?"

But she can't speak. Too busy crying out at my cock stretching her tight pussy, my thumb circling hard on her clit and driving pleasure through her limbs.

"I want to coat every inch of you. Your thighs, your pussy, your stomach, your tits, your pretty face. I want my cum in your throat, on your tongue. Dripping from your pussy and ass, leaking down your legs with every step."

She stiffens at the mention of my cum in her ass, but the pleasure is too consuming to formulate a protest. God, I love her this way. Entirely overcome by ecstasy. Wholly at my mercy.

Her pussy throbs, and I know she's close. So I pull out, finger disappearing from her swollen clit.

"What the hell?" she snaps. "Don't stop!"

"On your hands and knees, muse."

Briar quickly does as I instruct, desperate for her release and willing to do anything to get it.

"Are you going to come for me?" I purr, easing my tip past her tight walls.

"Yes!" she cries.

Her pussy gives a hard throb around my cock, but she's not there yet. I find her clit, pressing down and rubbing to help her climb to that height of ecstasy.

"Agh! That feels so fucking good!" she shouts, ass bouncing as I pound into her, her dripping pussy squelching with every thrust.

"Come for me, sinner."

Before the last word of the command leaves my lips, she's unraveling beneath me, arms giving out as she falls forward onto the mattress, ass still in the air as her pussy takes its pounding and she grips the bedsheet. Her screams are my symphony.

I slow my thrusts as she comes down from her orgasm, even as my abs clench and balls tighten, eager for my own release. Her fingers ease their grip on the sheet and she pushes herself up onto shaking hands.

"You're doing so well, muse." I slide out of her pussy, slipping a finger inside to replace it. She whimpers softly, and once my finger is coated, I drag it up between her ass cheeks.

She stiffens and starts to pull away from me. "Absolutely *not*—"

I stop her with a hand on her shoulder, finger motionless against her forbidden hole. "Do you trust me?"

Silence until she finally admits, "Yes, but—"

"If you trust me, you'll let me have your ass, Briar. You've allowed me to pleasure every other part of your body. Allow me to pleasure every inch."

Though I know she'll love it, I wait for her sigh of acquiescence. "Fine. We can try it. But the second our safe word is out of my mouth, you better fucking stop or I'll literally chop your dick off."

"That's what our word is for, muse."

I slip a second finger in her pussy to swipe the wetness up to her asshole, swirling the mess between her cheeks before slowly sinking a finger inside her. She stiffens, but she doesn't object.

"Relax."

At the order, she focuses on letting her tight muscles unravel. Her walls loosen around my finger, and I spit on her ass, pushing more lubricant inside her tight hole.

"Mmm." The moan leaves her throat unbidden.

"Yeah," I breathe, fucking her ass tenderly with my finger. "You're going to love this. You're going to love everything I give you and beg me for more."

"We'll see about that." But she's already groaning again.

Her sounds alone are nearly enough to make the cum spurt from my aching cock. I need to be inside her, but I have to get her ready first. I spit on my cock to add to the lubrication from her pussy. We both need to be lubricated enough to make this pleasant for her. Because I'm going to want to take her ass as often as I can after this.

I pull my finger out, playing with her clit to keep her relaxed and wet for me as I nudge my tip at her virgin hole.

She tightens beneath me again, bracing herself.

"Relax," I soothe again. "You know you can trust me."

She forces her muscles to loosen, focusing on the pleasure mounting from her swollen, abused clit.

Slowly, I push the tip of my cock into her ass.

I freeze, allowing her to acclimate to the foreign feeling of being stretched there. She breathes deeply, relaxing her tight muscles, and her walls slowly loosen to stretch around me.

"You're doing fucking incredible, muse."

"I know," she pants.

"Do you want the rest of my cock?"

"Yes." Her nails curl into the bedsheet again. "Fuck me."

"With pleasure." I groan as I slowly push every inch of my throbbing cock inside her ass. She cries out, not stopping until I bury my hard length to the hilt, her ass cheeks pressing against my pelvis.

"It's so big," she whimpers.

"I know."

She swings back to swat at me, but I'm out of reach and my cock filling her ass keeps her rooted in place.

I pull back just slightly before thrusting back into her, harder this time. She yelps and arches her back, but her clit throbbing beneath my finger tells me she loves everything I'm doing to her.

When I stop moving, she calls out, "Keep going."

This time, when I pull out, I leave only the tip in her ass before slamming back in. Her ass jiggles against me, and her whole body clenches as she screams.

Wetness drips from her pussy onto my hand rubbing her clit. Her arms give out again as she screams into the mattress, and I fully unleash myself on her, grinding my teeth and pounding her ass. The slap of skin on skin is nearly drowned out by her screams and my throaty groans.

As soon as her ass clenches on my cock and her pussy throbs in my hand as she comes, I allow myself to follow her. Every muscle in my body tightens before relaxing all at once as a load of cum spurts from my cock and fills her. My eyes roll and the roar that escapes my throat is loud even to my ears, unprecedented pleasure barreling through me.

"Saint! Oh my fucking god!"

She keeps coming after I've fully spilled inside her, screaming my name in unparalleled ecstasy as her entire body writhes.

My heart pounds, neck and back slick with sweat. My arms grow weak, and if I don't pull out soon, I may collapse on top of her, unable to move until dawn.

Once she's finally come down from her orgasm, and we're both panting and breathless, I slowly pull out of her, dragging some of my cum with me.

She collapses onto the mattress, utterly spent, and she's never been more beautiful. "Saint?"

I brush a strand of hair from her lips while she stares up at me from her prone position on the mattress with those big blue eyes. "Yes, muse?"

"I swear to god, if you break my fucking heart, I'll break you."

CHAPTER SEVENTEEN
BRIAR

I REREAD THE NOTE SAINT LEFT ON MY BED THIS MORNING. I vaguely remember him murmuring in my ear and pressing a kiss to my cheek on his way out the door.

Doing a little research. Will return soon with my findings.

This must have something to do with what he said last night about April. How apparently Saint believes she isn't my stalker even when the evidence is so blatant. Even after I've literally caught her following me around.

My ringtone blasts, making me jump. Trevor.

For a moment, my heart drops. What if this is Saint calling me from Trevor's phone after he killed him? He hates any man who glances my way, let alone a man I call a friend. A man who's been trying to help me get Saint thrown behind bars.

"Hello?" I croak into the phone.

"Hey, sorry. Did I wake you?"

I nearly collapse with relief at Trevor's voice on the other end. "Hey! No worries. I was already up."

I get that Saint wants to protect me, but Trevor's always been on my side. He has nothing to worry about.

"Oh, good. I needed you to hear this as soon as possible." A note of urgency tinges Trevor's typical easygoing tone. "Remember the footage you wanted me to get from the parking lot to see who vandalized your car?"

I sit up, tucking the blanket to my chin. "Yes?"

It must've been April. If we have video proof of her smashing the window on my car, I can take that to the police when I file a report about her stalking me. There's no way she'll get away with it now.

Trevor sighs like he knows I'm not going to like what he has to say. "It was your student. Saint de Haas."

My heart stops. I can't hear anything for a moment as a buzz drones in my head. "What? No. It can't be him. You must have the wrong guy."

Maybe the footage shows the vandal at a distance. A tall man who happens to share a similar stature to Saint. But it can't possibly be him because the Saint de Haas I know would never do something like that.

"I'm sorry. I know he got to you." Another sigh. "I hate that I have to be the one to tell you."

I shake my head. I don't care what Trevor thinks he saw—he's wrong. "There's no way the person who smashed the window was Saint. He wouldn't do that. He wants to protect me, not hurt me."

"Is that what he told you?" Trevor's tone is sympathetic now. "A man doesn't break into a woman's house to keep her safe, Briar. He's there to take. Whatever he wants."

My cheeks are burning even as I know in my gut that Saint can't be responsible. "I need to see the footage."

The distance probably distorts the image. Maybe it really is April, but the footage is too grainy. Even if Trevor can't properly identify her, I can.

"I'll get it to you as soon as possible," he promises.

My phone buzzes. A message from my stalker. My heart sinks. April is still after me, and I'm no closer to stopping her.

She sent me a video.

"Hey, can you hang on a second? My stalker just sent me a video."

"Oh, fuck. Maybe you shouldn't watch it." A note of wariness in Trevor's voice. "Who knows what it is."

He's right to be wary. My stalker has never sent me a video before. If I watch this, who knows what I'll see. But I can't ignore it. She sent me this video for a reason.

"I have to. Hang on." I mute myself before I click on the video.

The video displays a dark room, and when I turn up the volume, I regret it as the huffs and moans of a couple fucking in a chair fill my ears.

The man is filming, proudly displaying the woman straddling his lap and riding him. A blonde woman with her hair in a ponytail. A Roman nose, delicate jawline, slender build.

April Emmons.

Revulsion twists my stomach. She tips her head back to let out a whiny moan.

Did she fuck a man and ask him to film it just to send it to me? Why?

Right as I'm about to stop the video and delete it, the man she's riding points the camera at a mirror above their heads. Displaying their reflections.

He's wearing a mask.

S.T. Nicholson's mask.

Saint's mask.

In his office.

My stomach drops before giving a sickening churn.

That's Saint. Or maybe he's S.T. Nicholson this time. The masked, anonymous author with far more secrets to hide than his face.

He's completely unrecognizable to me now. I don't know this man.

Maybe I never really did.

Just last night, I let him in my bed. Let him in my body, let him use me exactly as he wanted.

And this is what he's doing to me now. A level of betrayal I never would've thought him capable of.

My heart splinters. I knew he was the last person I should love, trust. But I did anyway. I fell for my stalker, a serial killer, knowing exactly what he was capable of. And I fell anyway.

He fucked April. My other stalker. Maybe they've both been in on this all along, from the very beginning. That's how she got my address, my phone number.

She gave him pussy, and he gave her everything.

He fooled me into believing he did the same for me.

I hope you're right, Briar. I really hope he doesn't hurt you.

Trevor's been right all along. I was the idiot who fell for a stalker's pretty words. Who let him manipulate me into believing I was actually falling in love with him.

When all of it's been a lie.

That's why Saint said April isn't stalking me. He was covering for her. In the moments he wasn't with me, he was fucking her. Both of them probably cackling the entire time about all the things I let him do to me. How naive I was to fall for someone as dangerous and untrustworthy as a stalker in a mask.

Tears are sliding down my face by the time I finally register Trevor calling out to me, drawing me back from the horror show I just witnessed in Saint's office. "Briar! What's happening? What's in the video?"

"Him," I croak. "Fucking someone." I hang up.

For the first time, I finally understand Saint's inclination to murder. Mixing with the agony in my chest is a blazing rage like I've never felt before. Not even when I uncovered my father cheating on my mother. Not even when we learned he'd been unfaithful to her countless times before. Not even when I discovered Saint's masked, shadowy figure on my property for the first time.

I want to kill him. Kill her. Both of them. I want to line them up and slash both of their throats. Shoot a single bullet through their heads. Fuck the consequences. Fuck prison. At least if I was locked up, I'd know it was for a good reason.

Maybe it would even help ease the aching, open wound in my heart.

The video ends, the frame freezing on their reflections—April's back to the mirror and S.T. Nicholson's mask facing the glass as she's mid-bounce on his cock.

A tear slips down my cheek when I whisper the word to his reflection. "*Grave*."

CHAPTER EIGHTEEN
SAINT

HE SAID HIS NAME IS TREVOR.

Trevor James Hobart is a difficult man to track down. Even more so the Trevor he was ten years ago.

Thanks to his district attorney father, he managed to get several indiscretions buried, including a history of violating girls when he was a minor. A hidden file that was nearly impossible for Zayden to crack due to Trevor's age at the time.

But Trevor didn't stop after he became an adult. They rarely do.

He was fired from his last position at a police department in California for abusing his power with vulnerable women.

After our little run-in at the campus security office, I couldn't shake off the hunch that there was more to Trevor that Briar didn't know. April cemented my suspicions. He's obviously attracted to Briar, though she's entirely oblivious. And he wants her ten thousand miles away from me.

But there's far more to him than I suspected. Much worse.

Perhaps this information will be enough to convince Briar that her so-called friend is a menace to society, specifically to women like her. Alone, vulnerable, desperate. The blueprint of the type of woman Trevor targets.

But maybe his past won't be enough to convince her. I need proof of what Trevor is up to now.

He lives in an apartment, so he can't be causing too much trouble when he has neighbors sharing a wall with him. Unless this is another Dahmer situation.

After a little jiggling with my lock pick in my stolen maintenance staff uniform, I gain entrance into Trevor's cramped apartment. The space wouldn't appear so small if he didn't have so much shit. Like he attempted to move a full house of belongings into a one-bedroom apartment.

No stacks of stolen case files or murder boards on the walls. Not much of a detective then. In the bathroom, short hairs dust the sink and rest in the garbage can after he cut his hair and trimmed his beard.

The messy apartment becomes far more interesting when I find his bedroom. Crumpled up bed sheets, a bedside table littered with used tissues and an uncapped bottle of lube, dirty clothes strewn across the floor, tattered curtain drawn over the lone window. In the corner is a rickety desk with a laptop, brand new and entirely out of place. His most prized possession. Jackpot.

I know exactly what I'll find but still dread looking. What sort of pictures of Briar has he taken? What obscene photos and videos has he edited to replace them with her image?

He hasn't set up a new passcode on his laptop yet. All of his files are at my fingertips.

What I'm looking for isn't difficult to find—multiple folders filled with porn, which he surely cycles through every time he jerks off. But a disturbing pattern quickly emerges.

All of the women in the videos and pictures he's saved have dark brown hair and blue eyes.

Just like my muse.

I click out of the porn folders. There must be something more. His obsession with her can't end here.

That's when I find it. A folder called *Her*.

Throat constricting, I open it.

Images of a brunette flood the screen. All of them taken surveillance style when she clearly had no idea she was being photographed.

None of the backgrounds are familiar. None of them were snapped on the Auburn campus, outside Briar's house, or in town.

These photos were taken in a major city, dozens of other people around her at any given time. She's trying to blend into the crowd but watching over her shoulder. Aware that someone is out there looking for her.

The images are too blurry and distant to identify the woman, but I'm certain she isn't Briar.

Whoever she is, this is the woman who has captivated Trevor's mind. Briar just so happens to be the unlucky woman with the same shade of mahogany brown hair.

A few clicks through the metadata on the recent photos tell me he hasn't photographed this woman in two years.

My heart slams against my ribcage hard enough to bruise. Trevor did something to this woman.

And he intends to do the same to my muse.

At Briar's house, I pound on the front door to give her a chance to answer and pretend we're a normal, civilized couple before I resort to breaking in through a window.

She takes her time coming to the door, not at all hurried on by my booming, frantic knocks.

Her hair is unbrushed, untamed like her spirit. She's wearing her usual glower, but there's something different in her eyes this time. An animosity I don't recognize, even from our early days before she learned my true intentions.

At her side, her hands are clenched into fists. One containing her phone.

I barge past her, heart thumping wildly as I slam the door shut behind me. "Briar, I found—"

She swings at me.

I manage to jump out of the way, dodging her attack. Her teeth are bared as she aims a fist at my head, emitting a guttural scream.

"Briar, what the *fuck?*" I hold my hands up. No fucking clue what I did to deserve this.

"You picked the wrong fucking woman to mess with, motherfucker!"

When she swings at me again, I catch her wrist. "Mess with you? What are you talking about? What the hell's going on?"

"Don't play stupid!" she screeches, cheeks flushed with fury. "You fucked someone!"

"What are you talking about? When? Before I met you, yes."

Her nostrils flare. "And after."

I shake my head, jaw hard. "No. I wouldn't do that. You're the only woman I've wanted since I met you."

"Then explain this fucking video." She thrusts her phone into my hand.

On the screen, amateur porn plays, the woman emitting falsetto moans that any man experienced in pleasuring a woman can easily discern as fake.

My heart stammers when it becomes clear the video was filmed in the office in my rental. The man wearing my mask.

April Emmons is riding him.

What the fuck?

April covers too much of his body in the mirror to try to decipher the possible identity of the man behind the mask. Disguising his silhouette enough to convince my muse that I've betrayed her.

"That isn't me."

Briar rolls her eyes dramatically, snatching the phone back. "Right. I'm supposed to believe April broke into your house with some random guy, he put your mask on, and they fucked in your office. All to send me a video."

My temper flares. "I'm telling you that's exactly what happened."

Her laugh is short and mirthless. I step toward her, but she backs away, shaking her head as angry tears spill down her cheeks. My chest constricts. She's pulling away from me. I thought I was finally getting through to her, getting her to put her trust in me, and she believes I cheated on her.

"You must think I'm a fucking idiot." She lets out a heart-broken, maniacal laugh. "This is why you said April wasn't stalking me. You were covering for her because you're fucking her."

Another step toward my muse. Another step in retreat. Our new dance. "No. I didn't cheat on you, muse. You know I would never hurt you." Another step, and she doesn't back away this time, keeping her chin high. "I thought you said you trusted me."

"Trust you?" she scoffs. "Trevor was right—you brainwashed me, made me think I could overlook the bright red flags that were waving right in front of my fucking face. You actually made me believe you when you said you'd never hurt me. All so I wouldn't see it coming. But guess what, motherfucker? You won't win this game. I'm done playing. Trevor has the footage from the parking lot the day you broke the window on my car. You're out of your fucking mind if you think I'm letting you get away with all this shit."

I close the distance between us, and she swallows, bravery wavering as I loom over her. "*Trevor* doesn't have shit."

"He does. He has proof of what you've done." Briar shoves at my chest, attempting to push me away. And despite everything, the brush of contact makes me want to sweep her up into my arms and fuck her against the door.

"He can't have proof because I'm not the one who smashed your window," I growl, beyond sick of Dickhead Trevor.

I should've gotten rid of him the day I met him. Now he's a bigger problem than Professor Molester ever was.

This is how he hurt all those women. He manipulated them, made them believe he was harmless, trustworthy. Now he's doing the same to my muse.

"That wasn't me in the video, Briar. That was Trevor."

She barks a laugh. "Trevor? Really? You're trying to pin this on him now?"

I drag my hands through my hair, turning on my heel to pace before I scream in frustration. What the fuck do I need to tell her to convince her I wouldn't do something like this? How many more days of my life do I need to spend convincing her that I'm better than the man she thinks I am?

"Yes. April fucked him for information. That's how she got your address. You have no idea what that man is capable of, Briar. His father was a DA in California. He's been violating girls since he was a minor, and he was fired from a police department for abusing his power with vulnerable women. He has a folder full of pictures of a woman with dark brown hair just like yours. So yes, Trevor broke into my house, bribed April to fuck him, and sent the video to you to frame me. He wants us apart so he can have you for himself. You're the replacement for the woman he likely killed."

Her mouth morphs into a snarl. "That's ridiculous. He's never even expressed a modicum of interest in me. And now you're accusing him of being a *killer*? You're the murderer here."

"He's biding his time." My sharp tone only makes her eyes narrow further. "He's waiting until he's sure you'll give him what he wants."

She shakes her head. "I don't believe you."

Deep down, Briar has been waiting for me to prove that she's right about love. To disappoint her, to betray her, to verify the false belief she's always held—that I'll hurt her. That loving me isn't worth the risk.

I cross the room before she can run from me, grabbing her

arms and squeezing. My heart is fucking shattering, and I can't take the agony of it for another second. "I didn't do this to you, Briar. I don't know what I have to say or do to convince you, but I vowed I would never hurt you and I will never break a vow to you."

She trembles in my hands. The heartbreak in her eyes rips me apart, my own stinging with hot tears. This can't be fucking happening. We haven't come this far for her to turn her back on me now. To despise me.

"Let me go," she demands.

The knot in my chest tightens, but I do as she requests, even as the act of letting her go fractures my soul. "Tell me what I can do. Tell me how to fix this."

I'll do anything she asks. Drop to my knees and beg. Write her a hundred books. Give her the keys to Nicholson Manor. Hand her all the proof of Trevor's transgressions.

Anything.

Briar lifts her chin, blue eyes boring into me. "Let me kill you."

Silence falls between us. We stare at each other, unmoving.

After everything I've done for her, everything I've made her feel, every sacrifice I've made, this is how she wants to write our ending. Not dying of old age in bed together, holding hands as our souls leave our bodies behind for the afterlife. But here, in this house.

With a knife in her hand as she drags it across my throat.

When the fire raging in her eyes doesn't extinguish, I head for the kitchen. She's on my heels as I reach the block of knives and pull one free with a soft hiss.

She stiffens, edging back along the wall like she's going to make a run for it as I head in her direction.

"What the fuck are you doing?" Her voice shakes.

When I reach her, I stop and hold out the handle. "I told you if you wanted to kill me, I'd hand you the knife."

With a shaking hand, she takes it, staring down at the glinting blade.

If she kills me, it will be a merciful death. Because I can't imagine living another day without her. A life without my muse isn't one worth living.

"You're my everything. If I don't have you, I'm nothing. I said I'd give you anything you want. If you want my blood on your hands, you can spill it. If you want the light to leave my eyes, you can extinguish it."

Her hand trembles, the knife with it.

Her fantasies are flashing through her mind. Of spilling my blood. Of spilling April's. Getting revenge on those who've hurt her. A woman so tired of being hurt.

The handle slips from her fist, clattering to the floor.

Briar strides to the door, pausing with her hand on the knob without glancing back at me. "The next time I see your fucking face, you're leaving in handcuffs or a body bag. Get out of my house."

CHAPTER NINETEEN
BRIAR

MACK HASN'T LEFT MY SIDE SINCE I TOLD HER THE NEWS. She makes sure I eat, and she's banned me from my true crime documentaries and horror films. I'm on a sitcom-reruns, comfort-food diet that mostly consists of soups, my favorite pastas, chocolate, and mechanical laugh tracks.

Since I confronted Saint with the video and seriously contemplated stabbing him, my other stalker has gone silent. I guess Saint called April off. I'm not stupid enough to think my punches and knife-wielding were actually enough to scare him. They're simply biding their time before the next strike.

Or maybe they're done with me. Bored and ready to find another woman to terrorize.

Despite everything the two of them have done to me, it's the video of him fucking her that I can't get out of my head. The part of this whole mess that feels like someone plunging a dagger repeatedly into my heart.

Which is absolutely insane. Infidelity shouldn't be the worst part of being stalked. That's what this love shit does to you— makes you insane. Makes you believe you can trust the untrust- worthy. Love the unlovable.

Mack enters my bedroom carrying a stack of books and my favorite chocolates. I roll my eyes as she dumps the stash on my bed. "More gifts Saint left on your doorstep."

"Exactly what my father did after he cheated on my mother for nearly two decades." He thought some meaningless gifts could buy my mother's love, as if a woman's heart has a price tag.

"Are you sure that was Saint in the video, Briar?" Mack's brows furrow. "It really doesn't seem like something he would do—"

"Mack, we've already had this conversation. I'm done with him. I shouldn't have let it go this far in the first place."

She allows a short silence to fall between us until she tilts her head at the suitcase on my bed while I toss clothes inside at random. "Going somewhere?"

"The writing retreat, remember?"

A grimace pulls at the corners of her mouth. "You're still going?"

"No, I'm packing for fun."

"Will Saint be there?" she asks carefully.

"He's been coming to class and he's still letting us use Nicholson Manor for our retreat. So probably."

Seeing him in class every day has been its own special brand of torment. If he were halfway decent, he'd drop out and leave me the fuck alone. Not continue showing up where he knows I can't escape him, just so I can struggle through my lectures with his onyx eyes glued to me. He'd stop leaving gifts on my doorstep that remind me of him, that force Mack to bring him up when she knows his name is the last thing I want to hear.

But Saint de Haas is a stalker, a murderer, and a cheater. There's no sense in expecting him to be any form of decent.

"Do you think you'll be able to handle him being at the writing retreat?" Mack asks.

"I'm a grown-up. I can handle being around an ex if I need to be."

"But . . . he's not just an ex. You really loved him, Briar. I can tell."

As much as I hate to admit it, she's right. The worst part is, I'm not just mourning the loss of Saint—I'm mourning the loss of my favorite author. How will I ever be able to read an S.T. Nicholson book again after what happened between us? Every time I catch a glimpse of one of his book covers, the image of him fucking April in his mask will haunt me.

Not only did he take my heart with him, he took my favorite books.

"What I really love is cheese," I tell her.

Mack sighs and pulls a pair of shorts from my suitcase. "For the love of god, who taught you how to fold?"

I flop onto the bed, staring up at the ceiling while Mack folds the clothes neatly in my suitcase.

"You know I hate to say I told you so—" I start.

"Do you?" she quips.

"But I definitely fucking told you so."

"About what?"

"About all that love shit. It doesn't make your life better—it makes everything a thousand times worse. If I hadn't fallen for Saint, I could've gotten him locked up ages ago and I wouldn't be dealing with all this shit right now."

Mack abandons my clothes and takes my hand. "Don't think with your head for a second—think with your heart. You know Saint. Do you really think he would want to hurt you? Do you really think he'd do something like that?"

Of course I don't. But I also didn't think my father would be capable of cheating on my mother with multiple women. I didn't think Dr. Barrett would be capable of groping me in public. I didn't think Austin would be capable of human trafficking. I can't trust my heart or my gut or whatever instincts I'm supposed to have. My heart is what got me in this mess in the first place. My heart made me ignore logic and fall for my stalker.

I climb out of bed and continue packing. "I'm done listening to my heart."

Whatever's left of it.

CHAPTER TWENTY
SAINT

MY MUSE BELIEVES I'M CAPABLE OF CHEATING ON HER. After I've dedicated so much time to proving otherwise. Proving to her that I'm nothing like Warren Marshall or Austin Emmons or Charles Barrett. That I'm nothing like those horrible men. That I would do anything, sacrifice anything, for her.

Yet none of it was enough. She's never been so close and yet entirely out of reach.

I wish she'd plunged that knife into my heart. Wish she hadn't spared me. The agony of having had her and now being forced to live without her is excruciating.

Without an agent, without a book deal, my muse is all that matters now.

"Saint?" Zayden's voice crackles over the speaker in my car. I forgot I called him.

I'm in the parking lot at the Auburn Institute of Fine Arts. I'll never be able to stay away from her, but she doesn't want me around either. Relegated again to the shadows.

"She thinks I cheated on her," I tell him. "She refuses to speak to me. I don't know how to fix it this time."

Silence falls between us as Zayden considers. "You said she's your biggest fan, right?"

"Yes. She was." Saying the words out loud is torment. She's probably burned every copy of my books she can get her hands on.

"So what would your biggest fan want for your next chapter?"

I've always been able to get in my readers' heads. To envision what they would hope for in my next installment.

But this time, when it matters most, I draw a blank. "I don't know."

"Give her some time. Let her come to you. Try exercising some patience for once."

"Excellent advice."

As soon as I end the call, I race across campus to the faculty building. Fuck patience.

But I halt when I spot Trevor fucking Hobart monitoring the students from a bench.

The fury boiling in my veins is nearly enough to compel me to attack him right here on campus with dozens of witnesses. But I keep my hands relaxed at my sides and stride over to him as if we're about to have an amiable conversation.

He stiffens when I sit beside him and drape my arms over the back of the bench. "So you and April Emmons?"

"I don't know what you're talking about." His eyes are as flat as his tone.

"Did you forget her name or did you simply never ask?"

He moves to stand, but my hand lands on his shoulder, keeping him in place.

"There are consequences when you fuck with me, Trevor. Especially when you fuck with my future wife."

He barks a laugh. "Future wife? You're delusional. She's done with you." He leans closer, mouth curled into a snarl. "I know exactly what you've done, man. To Austin. To Dr. Barrett. You're the one who doesn't want to fuck with me. Watch yourself."

With that, he stomps off. His lies are almost convincing. No wonder Briar fell for his manipulations along with so many other women. No wonder she mistook him for a friend.

I brush past throngs of students and staff and beeline straight for her office.

I don't bother knocking before flinging the door open. Briar barely reacts, like she anticipated my arrival.

"Leave the door open," she instructs, monotone.

"That's not necessary."

Her electric blue gaze has already returned to the paperwork she's filling out. "If you don't want me to file a restraining order against you, it is. Trust me, the administration cares way more about their professors than a single student. You'll be banned from campus tomorrow."

I perch on her desk. "Will you still be hosting the writing retreat at Nicholson Manor?"

Briar's pen continues scrawling across the page. "Yes, I'll need to be there a day early to set up for the writing retreat. Will that be a problem?"

"Not at all." I grab her chin, forcing her fiery gaze on mine because I'm sick of her refusing to look at me. Her jaw ticks. "No matter how much you push me away, no matter how long you refuse to look me in the eye, I'll still do whatever I need to do to provide for you. To take care of you, to prove my loyalty and love for you."

She jerks out of my grasp, returning her attention to her desk. "Get out, Saint."

If she's at Nicholson Manor a day before her students, I can utilize that time to remind her of what our writing retreat was like over winter break. How happy she was with me, how much she trusted me, what it felt like to fall in love with me.

What would your biggest fan want for your next chapter? Perhaps this is her way of telling me what she wants me to write in our story next.

CHAPTER TWENTY-ONE
BRIAR

I MANAGE TO KICK MACK OUT OF THE HOUSE WHILE I finish prepping for the writing retreat. She's getting Cookie settled with Ginger at her apartment where she'll watch them while I'm gone for the week.

When there's a knock on the door, my stupid heart flutters with the hope that it's Saint on the other side.

But when I swing the door open, it's not Saint or Mack. "Trevor? What are you doing here?"

He grins and points past me. "Can I come in?"

"Uh, sure. But I can't talk long. I'm leaving for the retreat soon."

"No problem." He slides his hands in his back pockets, hovering in the middle of the room. "So I was thinking when you get back, I could take you out."

Oh, fuck. Where the hell is this coming from? Trevor and I have always been just friends. He's never shown any interest in me before.

Saint's words echo in my mind. *He's biding his time. He's waiting until he's sure you'll give him what he wants.*

Goddamnit. Why do men always have to ruin a perfectly

good friendship by catching feelings? Or, at the very least, wanting to bang any woman who is remotely pleasant to them.

"Oh. Um . . . that's nice of you to ask. It really is." God, I'm terrible at this. "But I'm not ready to date again. Honestly, I may never be."

At this point, I'd rather stab out my own eyeballs with a fork than suffer through a date with anyone.

Trevor's hands leave his pockets as he folds his arms, an unexpected scowl shifting his features. "Don't tell me you're still in love with that asshole."

Silence falls between us while I try to come up with a response that's anything other than telling him to fuck off. "I don't know if you've realized this, Trevor, but I've been through a lot of shit recently. I'm not interested in dating anyone."

He shakes his head, brushing past me on his way to the door. "You women love to complain about asshole guys, but you always pick them over the nice guys. You could date a guy like me who would actually treat you right, but instead, you're hung up on a scumbag who stalked you. I guess I should try being more like him, huh? Maybe if I start treating women like shit, you'll all start liking me better."

I'm finally meeting the real Trevor. The one Saint told me about. The man who manipulates and takes advantage of women. Who pretends to be your friend until he turns on you when you reject him, and that's when he shows his true colors.

"Were you the one in that video?"

His eyes narrow on me, hand frozen on the knob. "How would it have been me? You said it was a video of him fucking someone."

"The man in the video was wearing a mask."

"So you think I played dress up with a mask and fucked some random girl?"

When he says it like that, it does sound fucking crazy. But maybe Trevor's fucking crazy. I don't know what to think anymore. "Not some random girl. April Emmons, Austin's sister.

The girl who thinks I killed her brother and mysteriously showed up at my house after someone gave her my address."

Trevor lets out a short laugh. "And why the hell would I do all that?"

"To drive me away from Saint." My voice shakes. "To make me believe the worst about him so I wouldn't want him anymore."

Saint might've been right. Maybe Trevor did all of this to drive us apart so he could swoop in and be the hero. The hero always gets the girl, after all. He's an ex-cop and a security guard —he's used to playing the hero.

I trusted him. Confided in him. Fed him all the information I knew about Saint. If he's the one behind all of this, if he's been using everything against me—

"The worst should've been him *stalking* you." He rolls his eyes. "And no, I didn't fuck Austin's sister while wearing a mask. You women are insane."

Maybe I shouldn't believe him. But I don't know how to believe either of them without solid proof.

"Where's that footage you said you had? Of Saint breaking the window on my car? You never showed it to me." How convenient that Trevor claimed to have video evidence, but it mysteriously hasn't materialized.

He shrugs. "Why would I bother now? All the evidence has been right in front of your face the whole time and you've ignored it."

Rage boils in my veins, and I'm done playing nice. "You know what the problem is with guys like you, Trevor? The *nice* guys like you are actually just the asshole guys in disguise. You think just because you're nice to a girl, she owes you something. You think showing a woman basic decency makes you a good guy, but you're not doing any of it because you're actually a good person. You're doing it to manipulate her into fucking you. Which makes you just as bad as the rest of them. I'd rather take a stalker who's at least honest about who he is and what his intentions are than a phony who's faking his personality to get laid."

Trevor stares at me for a few moments, fire burning in his eyes. I've hit my mark. I only wish I'd seen Trevor's true colors sooner. "You're just as fucking crazy as he is."

I smile sweetly at him. "That's exactly what a nice guy would say. Now please get the fuck out of my house."

CHAPTER TWENTY-TWO
BRIAR

WHILE WE'RE PACKING MY CAR FOR THE WRITING RETREAT, Mack sighs wistfully. "So I know I said I was just going to help you unpack and set up, but I think I'm going to stay for the week. I'll totally be out of your way. You won't even know I'm there. Just tell me if there's a hot tub so I can bring a swimsuit."

"This is not a vacation—this is work. And the cats need you or they'll starve." Sunlight reflects off my car as I open the trunk with a squeak and heave my suitcase inside. Thick gray clouds promising heavy rain are swiftly moving in.

Mack rolls her eyes. "They would never starve. They'll figure out how to open doors to get to their food and catnip. They'll be happier than they've ever been."

"And then you'll come home to shit all over your house."

She chews on her lip. "Maybe I can hire someone to dig the shit out of their litter boxes."

Near the end of my driveway, a black BMW parks along the sidewalk.

You've got to be shitting me.

"Who's that?" Mack asks.

"April Emmons. The girl who's been stalking me and fucked Saint." Possibly. Unless it was Trevor. I have no idea anymore.

Mack's eyes practically pop out of her head. "Oh shit," she mutters as April climbs out of her car and strides toward us.

"What the hell do you want?" I call when April's halfway up my driveway.

This time, she's not confronting me with fire raging in her eyes, and I finally notice how young she is. Twenty-two, still in law school, and searching for whoever gave her brother the drugs that killed him.

She stops a few feet away, biting her lip. "Your boyfriend isn't the one in that video."

I play dumb. "What video?"

April rolls her eyes, trying to manage her impatience with me. "The video of me with the masked man."

I stuff a bag with writing supplies into the backseat. "Stop covering for him. It's already over."

"I'm not." April steps forward, holding out her phone. "I have proof. And to be honest, I wouldn't want to cover for him anyway. He was an ass."

My heart leaps into my throat. I so badly want to believe her. Want to see the proof that Saint wasn't the man behind the mask that night. But I push the inkling of hope back down. "So why do you care?"

"I don't. I want to know the truth. I'll show you the proof if you tell me whether you gave Austin those drugs."

I approach her slowly. Her gaze tracks my movements warily until I grab her hand. She's scared and alone, searching for the answers she's desperate for.

Even after everything, I can't bring myself to tell her Saint gave Austin the coke. She likely wouldn't believe me anyway, and there's nothing tying him to the crime. But I can tell her what she wants to know.

"I swear I didn't give him those drugs, April."

Her eyes shimmer, but she doesn't pull away. "I hate that I believe you."

For the first time, I put myself in her shoes, and I can understand. If I thought some random woman overdosed someone I love, I'd do everything in my power to bring them justice too.

Mack glances back and forth between me and April. "Um, sorry, but if it's not Saint in the video, who is it?"

"Right." April sniffles and clicks on her screen before turning it toward me and Mack.

The same video I got in the text plays. I don't want to watch this shit again. "I've already seen this."

"He trimmed the video. Keep watching," April insists.

After the same first thirty seconds pass, the video continues. In it, the man behind the mask murmurs, "Better keep your mouth shut if you don't want anyone to see this."

Beside me, Mack stiffens.

His voice is distorted behind the mask, but it doesn't sound like Saint's.

In the video, April reaches for S.T. Nicholson's mask. My heart is about to burst. Every last bit of hope in my body is screaming for it to be anyone but Saint.

April lifts the mask off his face. Displaying his reflection in the mirror.

Trevor.

My stomach hits the ground.

"That asshole!" I screech.

Saint was right. Trevor was framing him. Fucking April and sending me the video to split us up.

And it worked.

Everything makes sense now. Once Trevor realized I was falling for Saint, he took it upon himself to scare me. To make silent phone calls and send me creepy texts and smash my window so I would believe Saint was behind it. So that I would fall out of love with him.

So I would want Trevor instead.

Nausea rolls in my stomach. This whole time, he's been pretending to help me, when in reality, he was the one behind all the psychological torment.

That's why the stalking stopped. Trevor got what he wanted.

"Oh my god," Mack whispers, hand covering her mouth. She's ghostly pale.

Saint wasn't lying. He didn't cheat on me. He didn't betray me. He vowed to never hurt me, and yet, at the first chance anyone gave me to doubt him, I did. I believed Trevor over Saint.

The biggest mistake I've ever made.

Saint has admitted to murdering men. Why would he have lied about infidelity?

My heart pounds. He loves me. He never did anything to hurt me. But he still handed me the knife when I wanted to kill him.

He would've made that sacrifice. For me.

All I want to do now is run to him and fall to my knees begging for forgiveness.

"How did you know I thought it was Saint in the video?" I ask April around the lump in my throat. "How did you even know Trevor sent this to me?"

"He showed up at my house yesterday." She clutches her arms across her middle. "I nearly threw up seeing him there. When we met, he told me he was a cop and offered to give me your address if I fucked him. He took the video to blackmail me so I wouldn't say anything to anybody. When he showed up at my place, he said you rejected him, even after the video convinced you it was Saint." She bites her lip. "Then he told me he's going to take care of your little boyfriend."

"*Oh my god*," Mack whispers again.

"Fuck." I rake my hands through my hair. Trevor could be going after Saint right now.

I scramble for my phone, hands shaking as I find Saint's number.

The phone rings. And rings. "Shit!"

Shit, shit, shit. What if Trevor has already found him?

Mack is so pale, April's eyes widen. "Is she going to faint?"

I grab my best friend's shoulders. "Mack, listen. Everything's going to be okay. But I need to go to Nicholson Manor. I know Saint will be there. I need to warn him."

I need to tell him that I'm still in love with him. That I've never stopped, even when I longed to hate him.

Mack's pale blue eyes are round when she murmurs, almost imperceptibly, "How do you know James?"

April's brows draw together. "Who's James?"

"Her ex," I explain, more confused now than ever. "What do you mean, Mack? I've never met James."

She jabs at April's phone, hand trembling. "That was James in the video."

"You mean Trevor?" April asks.

"He's the security guard on campus." My heart pounds against my ribcage in the ensuing silence.

Mack fights back tears. "That's James. Trevor James Hobart. When I knew him, he went by James."

My head swims, trying to process her words. What this means.

Trevor is the ex Mack fled California to escape. The ex-cop she couldn't report to the authorities because they refused to take action against one of their own. The ex who abused and terrified her so badly, she decided it was safest to disappear.

The ex who stalked her. Who tried to kill her.

James.

Trevor James Hobart.

CHAPTER TWENTY-THREE
SAINT

I'm certain Briar told me about her plan to be at Nicholson Manor a day early so I'd meet her there. Deep down, she wants to be together, even if she's still in denial. Even if she's terrified of risking her heart.

Her favorite gifts on her doorstep haven't swayed her. I need to remind her what life is like with me, how happy she is when we're together. Starting with a romantic dinner, followed by a candlelit bath, and an evening of reading together by the crackling fireplace. Whatever she wants, whatever she asks of me, I'll give to her.

Fortunately, her car isn't in the driveway yet when I pull in. I still have time to set up.

I will do anything to get her back. To keep her forever. Anything.

My footsteps echo through the silent manor. From a seat at the dining room table, the intruder smiles.

My stomach plummets to my feet.

"S.T. Nicholson. Where's your mask?" He nudges a glass of scotch toward me, nodding for me to take a seat at my own table.

I thought I'd need to find him, but it seems he's chosen to make my job easier. "Hello, Trevor. Come to chase Briar through my manor again? Or watch us fuck in the sunroom, perhaps?"

His lip curls up with distaste. "Not this time."

"To what do I owe the pleasure then? Come to fuck another woman in my office? I'm afraid my mask is in the car."

"I won't be needing it. The only woman I'll be fucking here is Briar."

Fury swiftly boils in my veins and I pat my waistband, heart dropping when I don't feel my gun in its holster.

I hadn't anticipated his arrival here. A stupid mistake.

One that may prove fatal.

"I'm sure your girlfriend would be unhappy to hear about that," I manage.

Trevor leans forward, mouth curdled in an ugly sneer. "She was just some whore who put out for a little information. She did a job, and she did it well—Briar finally realized she shouldn't be with a lunatic like you."

I take the seat across from him, trailing a lazy finger around the rim of the scotch. "You know, impersonating a police officer is illegal. Still abusing your power even after being forced to turn in your badge, I see." I lean back when he doesn't respond. "She's twenty-two. Her brother just died. Vulnerable, desperate. You took advantage."

His dark chuckle claws down my spine like talons. "So the serial killer is going to lecture me on what's illegal?"

I stiffen. How much has Briar told him? Regardless, he has no proof. Nor will he be leaving my home alive to tell the tales of my criminal activity. "I don't coerce and blackmail women."

"No, you only stalk them." Trevor takes in the high ceiling and towering dark walls of Nicholson Manor. "Can't imagine what a *bestselling author* could want with an MFA program. But I suppose your work could use some improvement."

I lift a brow. "You've read my work?"

"Unfortunately. Briar wouldn't stop going on about your latest book." His mouth sours.

I lift the glass to my lips. "Not to your taste?"

"Let's just say it was the worst drivel I've ever read in my life."

Drivel.

This is my friend's favorite book so I decided to give it a try. This is the worst drivel I've ever read in my life.

The first line of the negative review that initiated my downward spiral.

That led me to miss my deadlines, get fired by my agent, and lose my book deal.

I sputter into my scotch, failing to swallow a drop. The bottom of the glass cracks when I smack it back down, liquid sloshing over the edge. "Was three thousand words not enough to adequately express your disdain for the book? You've come here to share your opinion to my face?"

He snickers. "I don't give a shit about your stupid book. I've come here to make sure you stay away from Briar."

"I thought your video already accomplished that."

"That's what I thought. Until she rejected me, and I realized she's still under your sick spell. So it seems like I'll have to get rid of you to free her from it."

Without my pistol in my waistband, the closest weapon is hidden near the front doors. The buzzing in my ears drones louder as my pulse quickens. "And how exactly do you plan to accomplish this?"

A sickening smile sweeps across his face, nodding down at my scotch. "You tell me, Author. You wrote it."

This Book Will Haunt You. A novel with one of my most controversial endings—the struggling writer is poisoned by his biggest critic before being buried alive.

Trevor poisoned my scotch.

My heart thuds harder. "If I recall, you referred to my ending as 'cheap' and 'predictable.'"

"And now you're experiencing it for yourself. You see it now, right? But hey, who am I to rewrite your work? This is your life, and you're the author. And if that doesn't do the trick." He pulls up his shirt to reveal a pistol on his hip. "I brought a backup plan."

Fuck. *Fuck, fuck*—

"Who was the woman in the photos? The one you followed around California." The words drag from my mouth, limbs growing limp.

"My soulmate." His throat bobs. "I've already lost Mack. I'm not losing Briar too. I'm sure as hell not losing her to someone like you."

"Mack?" With the last dregs of my energy, my gaze flashes up to his.

Mack. Briar's best friend. My personal assistant. With blue eyes that are an eerie match to Briar's. A natural brunette before she bleached her hair.

The images of her on Trevor's computer were too blurry to identify her.

She managed to escape him. Until he tracked her to Maine. Unable to find her when he finally arrived.

That's why he chose Briar. He couldn't find Mack, so he tried to take the best replacement he could find.

My pulse is slowing from its breakneck speed as I grind the words out. "If you . . . loved her . . . why did you . . . hurt her?"

Trevor's fist squeezes around the glass in front of him. "You have no idea what the fuck I did or didn't do to her. I loved her. More than you've ever loved anyone."

I manage a breathy chuckle. "If you . . . loved her . . . you would've been . . . faithful to her. To your grave."

Briar will realize that someday. That I was loyal to her every moment since I met her. Even if that revelation doesn't come until after I've taken my final breath.

"Speaking of graves." Trevor rises, chair grating across the floor. "Briar is too blind to see how much better I am for her while you're still around." He approaches as my eyes fall shut. "So there's only one solution to that, isn't there?"

CHAPTER TWENTY-FOUR

BRIAR

FUCKING TREVOR.

Of course he's the one behind all of this. Typical "nice" guy controlling his girlfriend and tracking her down across the country.

When he couldn't find Mack, he found me—my resemblance to her uncanny. I became a decent substitute to the real thing until he realized I'd never feel the same way. Now he's doing the only thing men like him know how to do in the face of rejection: retaliate.

I call Saint again.

The phone rings. And rings.

No answer.

Fuck. We may already be too late.

"Do you want me to call the police?" April offers.

"No!" Mack and I shout in unison.

Officer Dan was on Trevor's side through all of this. Feeding him information, trying to convince me to make an official report. Probably so they could twist my words and implicate Saint in all of this.

Saint claims he has a weapon for each of his enemies stashed in Nicholson Manor. He's murdered three men. He can defend himself.

If April sends the police to Nicholson Manor, they'll discover Saint standing over Trevor's dead body, covered in his blood.

Unless Trevor ambushes him.

Or James. Whoever the fuck he is.

I hope Saint hasn't killed him yet so I can deliver the final blow. I want to watch the light leave that motherfucker's eyes. For everything he did to my best friend. For all the shit he's put us through.

If anyone deserves to rot in hell, it's Trevor James Hobart.

"You go," I tell April. "Go home."

"Please delete that video." For the first time, her gaze is pleading. "That can't get out."

"It won't," I promise her. "I'll delete it. And we'll delete it off Trevor's phone too."

"How are you going to do that?"

"Don't worry about it," I snap. "Just *go*, April. I need to get to Saint."

Who knows what's happening on that mountain. But if Saint could, he would've answered my calls.

He needs me. And I need him. I can't let him believe for one more second that I don't love him.

He vowed that there was nothing he wouldn't do for me. Now it's my turn to make that vow to him.

April nods, rushing for her car.

Dark clouds blot out the blue sky. But even a torrential downpour won't keep me from Saint de Haas. If the roles were reversed, he wouldn't let a little rain stop him.

He would do everything he could to get to me. To protect me.

I grab Mack's trembling hands. "I need to go to Saint. You stay here, okay?"

She shakes her head quickly. "No way. I'm not letting you go by yourself."

"And I'm not letting you anywhere near that asshole again."

Mack has spent the past two years hiding from Trevor. If I bring her up that mountain, all of that time will have been for nothing. All of the sacrifices she made, the time she went without seeing her own family, the entire life she gave up for refuge—all of it will be wasted if she walks right back into his waiting arms.

If he gets his hands on her because of me, I'll never forgive myself.

"Don't go without me. I don't want to be alone, Briar." Her bottom lip wobbles. "I don't want him to find me alone."

I wrap my arms around her and squeeze her to me. My heart breaks at the fear in her voice. I want to slice a fresh wound into his skin for every time he hurt her.

I have to go to Saint. I can't let Trevor hurt him. But I also can't leave Mack behind.

"He won't. I won't leave you alone." When I pull back, I force my voice to brighten. "It's one of him against three of us. Saint has a manor full of weapons, and he's killed before. If he needs to, he can do it again."

She nods. "We need to do this. *I* need to do this." Her eyes flood with tears until they're spilling down her cheeks. "I'm done running from him. I don't care what the outcome is—if he goes to prison or a grave. I just want this to be over."

I take her hand, my own eyes misting at her tears. "Are you sure?"

This is her last chance to stay here. To keep hiding somewhere safe. And no matter the outcome, no matter who comes back down that mountain, Mack will be okay as long as she stays hidden.

If she comes with me to Nicholson Manor, I can't guarantee her safety. Any of ours.

I can't guarantee our survival.

"Yes. We're in this together." She squeezes my hand. "Sisters."

That's what makes this so much harder. Mack is my best friend, the closest thing I've ever had to a sister, and now I'm leading her into the lion's den.

"Besides, you need me. I've got this." She lifts her shirt to reveal a pistol in a holster on her hip.

I gasp. "Where the hell did you get that?"

"I applied for my pistol permit after I had that nightmare about James killing me." She bites her lip. "I wanted to feel like I could protect myself."

I suppose it's a good thing she did. Now she may have to use it.

My heart is in my throat when we climb into the car. I've never been scared of Trevor before, but now that I know his true identity, now that I know he's always been the James from Mack's nightmares, terror thrums through my veins.

He claimed to love Mack, yet he intentionally hurt her. Over and over.

If he can do that to someone he claims to love, what is he capable of doing to someone he hates?

I won't be able to live with myself if something happens to Saint. Or if Trevor gets his hands on Mack again.

I need to do everything I can to stop him.

Behind the wheel, I slam on the gas. "Let's get this motherfucker."

CHAPTER TWENTY-FIVE
SAINT

Trevor drags my limp body outside. Fresh spring grass hisses beneath my weight, Trevor huffing and grunting as he pulls me by the feet.

As I suspected, those muscles are simply for show. He can deadlift three hundred pounds in a single rep, but dragging a one-hundred-eighty-pound body is a struggle. He's not cut out for this life of crime.

No neighbors. No one to see us. No one to hear the gunshot if he decides to ensure I'm dead.

He has two options: hide my body where no one will find it until the cause of my death can no longer be determined, or bury me.

I hope he's stupid enough to hide my body in the woods.

Whatever he chooses, neither will keep me from her.

When Trevor drops my feet and metal clinks against dirt, I dare a glance at my surroundings.

Headstones border us, the cemetery particularly eerie at dusk. In the gravel drive up to the open gate, a truck sits parked. That's how Trevor hid his vehicle from me when I arrived at Nicholson Manor.

Microscopically, I turn my head to the left. To face my fate.

161

Trevor spears a shovel into a mound of dirt beside a large hole. A vacant spot away from the other headstones.

He dug a grave. But that's not all that awaits me.

Inside is a coffin. My heart sinks.

I squeeze my eyes shut, trying to wrap my head around how I'll escape this.

If he realizes he failed to drug me, that I recognized what he was planning the moment I lifted the scotch to my lips and returned it to the table without taking a sip, he'll point his gun at me instead. And that I won't survive.

"It didn't have to be this way," Trevor croons to what he assumes is my drugged, unconscious body. "You could've kept playing the villain, and I could've been the hero. But you had to go and screw it up. You took her away. You fucked her, brainwashed her into falling in love with a psychopath."

With his foot, he rolls my limp body into the coffin, biting back a grunt as my heart jackhammers while I debate the right next move. Play my hand now, jumping up only for him to shoot me before I can get to her.

Or allow him to bury me alive, and hope that I can claw my way back out, to reach her before he does.

"Luckily, you gave me plenty of time to prepare this for you. A private cemetery with no visitors. A groundskeeper who was too afraid to make the trek up the mountain." The lid creaks as he shuts me in. "Now you finally know how your story ends."

CHAPTER TWENTY-SIX

BRIAR

My heart pounds the entire drive back to Nicholson Manor. What if Trevor has already beaten us there? What if Saint is on the floor, bleeding out, unconscious, and past the point of saving?

What if I'll never get to apologize or tell him I love him? That I've been in love with him for a while, but I refused to admit it even to myself.

He already knows. But he deserves to hear me say it.

When we speed into his driveway, Saint's car is the only one parked there. "Maybe Trevor isn't here," I say, heart leaping with hope.

Maybe we're not too late. If Saint simply slept through my calls, I'll be equal parts pissed and relieved.

Beside me, Mack visibly relaxes. We're going to be okay. But I still need to make sure Saint is all right.

I've barely thrown the car in Park when I jump out.

"Holy. Fucking. Shit." Mack smacks my arm. "You two have been hiding this fucking *fortress* up here?"

"Not important right now, Mack!" When I run halfway to the manor, Mack stays rooted in place, chewing her lip and face paling again as she imagines the horrors she could face inside.

"You can stay in the car. Lock it. Hide in the trunk or something."

She shakes her head. "No. I'm coming with you. If he's here, we're ending this. For good."

I race for Nicolson Manor, Mack on my heels. "Saint! *Saint!*" I throw the door open, the mansion eerily still and uninhabited. "Saint!"

Mack is my shadow as we fly up the stairs. "This is his *house?*"

We sprint through room after room, this manor way too fucking big to find anyone quickly. Despite the adrenaline coursing through my veins, I'm already breathless, heart racing toward collapse.

We're clearly alone in here. Part of me is relieved Trevor isn't waiting in ambush. Another part of me is terrified about what this silent, empty manor could mean for Saint.

When we finally stop in his room, he's not asleep in bed as I hoped. My chest squeezes painfully.

We bend at the knees and heave. Mack pants, "Maybe . . . he's not in here. Should we . . . look outside?"

"Yeah," I huff. "Let's go."

"Wait." She stops me with a hand on my arm. "Do you smell that?"

She's right. There's a weird scent in the air—something pungent and acrid.

My stomach drops.

Smoke.

I race to the enormous floor-to-ceiling windows, but there isn't a fire raging outside in the creeping darkness.

Fuck. That can only mean—

"We need to get out of here." I grab Mack's hand, and we race from the room and down the flights of stairs until we reach the massive foyer.

A raging fire consumes the front doors.

The overwhelming stench of gasoline mixes with the smoke

billowing into my lungs. Mack coughs violently beside me.

"I've been looking for you for a long time."

Both of our hearts stop at the sound of Trevor's bone-chilling voice behind us.

I grab Mack's hand as we spin, squeezing it gently to reassure her. I won't let this motherfucker get his hands on her again.

When her gaze lands on him, she takes an involuntary step back, hanging onto my hand for dear life.

I hate that she's gotten roped into this. That she has to face him again.

"You're blonde now." He steps closer, and I stand in front of her, shielding her from him.

"Don't talk to her. Don't even look at her."

"Why did you leave me, Mack?" His voice actually cracks like he's somehow the victim in all this.

That's what's so dangerous about men like Trevor. They never see the true villain in the mirror.

"Because you hurt her. You tried to kill her, asshole!" I snap.

Mack's hand trembles in mine. "How did you find me?"

He takes another step forward, his voice eerily tender in a way I've never heard before. "It took a lot of digging and bribery. A lot of searching through surveillance cameras and tracking your stops at different ATMs. Eventually, I found out you ended up somewhere around Auburn, Maine. But even after we were in the same city, I couldn't find you." A watery smile crosses his face. "Until now."

Silence falls around us as Mack takes another step back, too terrified to speak.

"Why did you come after me?" I demand. I already know the answer, but I need to hear him say it. Confess to all his sins.

His gaze snaps to me, like he's finally registering my existence. "Look at you two. You could be sisters. She had your hair, before she left. Before she disappeared."

Before she bleached it to hide from him.

"You followed me here, didn't you? When I went on a

writing retreat for a month. You couldn't stand not knowing where I was that long. That's when you watched through the window while Saint fucked me."

His mouth curls into a snarl, churning the bile in my gut. "You had a crazed stalker on the loose. Of course I had to know where you were. Then I saw him fucking you . . ." He squeezes his eyes shut. In that moment, it was probably Mack he saw on that table with Saint. "That's when I knew for sure he'd gotten to you. So I had to make you see reason."

All of the pieces of this horrible, gruesome puzzle click together. The smoke is thickening now, drifting up to the towering ceiling. Behind me, Mack wheezes.

"So you waited until he left me alone. And you cut the power and chased me through the manor."

"I needed you to realize how dangerous he is. I needed to get you away from him."

"All because I look like Mack."

Silent tears are falling down her cheeks now, her hand squeezing mine so hard, my fingers tingle. But I'm not letting her go.

His beady eyes drift back to Mack behind me. "I thought I'd lost you forever. That I was too late. I thought you were dead." His voice cracks and I want to smack him for daring to act heartbroken about Mack's death when he wanted to kill her himself. He holds out his hand to her. "Now I've finally found you again. We can be together."

He's out of his fucking mind.

Mack steps up beside me, squaring her shoulders and lifting her chin even as she continues to shake. "I'm not going anywhere with you, James. I'm done."

In seconds, his eyes morph from gentle and hopeful to cold and empty. The same way they did when I rejected him.

The abrupt shift sends a glacial chill down my spine.

"You can choose to go with me or I can take you. Those are your options."

"The hell they are—"

"No." Mack's voice is hard as concrete, silencing both of us. "You can be in prison or dead, James. Those are *your* options."

She drops my hand to grab the gun on her hip.

Trevor lunges for her, both of us screaming as he rips us apart. Trevor shoves me, and my ass hits the floor.

My heart gallops as I jump back up, refusing to let him take her away from me. Over my dead fucking body.

I slam into his arm, trying to get her free of him, grabbing for her shoulders. "Mack, run!"

But something hard strikes me in the side of the head. Fireworks burst in my skull.

I hit the floor, vision spinning and head throbbing as unconsciousness draws near. Unable to do anything other than listen to the crackling fire crawling toward me and Mack screeching my name. "*Briar!*"

Pain lances through my temple and I groan, barely able to roll onto my back.

Mack lets out a bloodcurdling scream.

He's got his hands on her.

Trevor wraps his arms around her like a straightjacket while she screams and thrashes.

"Leave . . . her . . . alone," I gasp out around the agonizing pain in my head.

But neither of them hear me over Mack's wails. Her arms are pinned at her sides. She tries to kick out at him, but he doesn't budge.

Fuck. I should've made her stay behind. I should've kept her safe; I should've protected her.

"Don't do this, James!" she yells. "Why do you think I left? I don't want to be with you!"

Trevor shakes her, even as his voice comes out soothing. "This is a fresh start for us, baby. Call me Trevor now."

As he drags her out of the house, the last thing I hear before my vision goes dark is Mack's scream.

CHAPTER TWENTY-SEVEN
SAINT

Trevor made one crucial mistake—he only read one of my books. If he'd read my debut, he'd know that the hero escapes being buried alive in the first chapter. Sometimes, the research an author does comes in handy.

I keep my breathing slow and steady to ration the limited oxygen. I brace my feet on the lid of the coffin, grateful Trevor was stupid enough to choose a flimsy option for my burial.

With one hard kick, my feet break through the bottom of the lid.

Dirt begins pouring in and collecting at my feet. I break the lid apart slowly, keeping the dirt at my sides while I gradually rise to sit.

At last, the lid is crumpled entirely, my escape somewhere above the feet of dirt.

I'm coming, muse. I won't let him hurt you. I'll protect you. I'll keep you safe.

He will never part me from her. He will never take her from me.

This is not the end of our story. We have several more chapters left to write. Whole novels, a series of installments of our adventures together. We have gardens to grow, books to write, countries to visit, food to taste, love to make.

Our story begins when that ring is on her finger and our vows leave our lips. *I do.*

Trevor will have to do a lot worse than bury me alive to stop me from crawling back to her. From spending the rest of my life with her until we're old and gray. Until we're nothing but dust.

I dig my way through the dirt until a muffled sound makes me pause.

Over the hiss of the earth shifting around me comes the patter of rain.

Fuck. My research for this chapter in my novel was thorough —wet dirt will be much more difficult to claw my way through. Heavy and compact, a near-superhuman strength required to push through it.

My limbs grow weak as the panic rises. Briar is still out there. Trevor is on his way to her. And I may be stuck here for hours.

For good.

My breaths turn shallow, head growing lighter.

Calm the fuck down. You can't protect her if you die here.

Maybe Trevor was right. This is how my story ends.

And Briar's . . . I don't want to imagine her next chapter without me. A vulnerable target to a crazed man who's gotten away with so many crimes before.

Her next chapters were supposed to be joyous. She'd find her name in the dedication of my next book, and she'd become my wife. She'd move into Nicholson Manor with me, surrounded by books she could spend every day reading to her heart's content. We'd write side by side, inspiring each other to pen every page.

My mother's voice, years since I last heard it, fills my ears. The stories she'd read to me before bed, her requests to hear the stories I wrote for her, her certainty that I'd write a book one day.

Meeting Briar. Hearing her passion for my books. Grabbing

the pan from her hand when she swung it at me. Dodging her fist when she aimed it at my face. Savoring the ecstasy that made her eyes roll and mouth fall open in a moan. Grinning when her musical laugh enveloped my heart. Rejoicing when she defended me, fought for me, showed her love for me even when she couldn't voice it. Watching her feelings for me shift from fear to trust. From hate to love.

She's all that matters. I can't die without convincing her that I did nothing to hurt her. That everything I ever did was to protect her, love her, keep her safe, make her happy.

Through the dirt above my head and the rain turning torrential, a muffled, high-pitched scream reaches my ears.

Briar. My muse.

My heart stops. He has her. He's going to hurt her.

I need to get to her. I cannot stop until I do. Until I rip her from his hands.

My racing heart slows. I'm not digging my way out of this grave for me. I'm doing this for her.

She needs to know. Everything I do is for her.

I need to hear her laugh again. Her voice. Her sarcasm. Her taunts. Her moans. Her defiance.

I need to hold her again. I need to be with her, even if my body gives out the second I get her in my arms again.

With each shift of the loose dirt around me, I hear Briar's voice.

Are you following me?

This is my favorite book. By my favorite author.

He writes in a way that makes me feel understood. Like in a way no one else in the world ever has.

S.T. Nicholson feels like a kindred spirit. Like if we met, we would just get each other.

I swear to god, if you break my fucking heart, I'll break you.

As insane as it makes me, yes. I want to come back and be here. With you.

No man has ever believed in me like you have or loved me like you have.

I want to do something to make your life better the way you've done for me.

Saint.

Saint.

Saint.

Loose dirt shifts only for more to replace it, the earth growing increasingly more difficult to move as the rain seeps in.

I'm coming for you, muse. I will not stop until I'm holding you in my arms again.

Trevor Hobart will not be the end of us. I won't allow it.

Saint.

Saint.

Saint.

Wet dirt sticks under my fingernails as I finally breach the surface, gasping for air. Limbs too weak now to run, walk, even stand.

But I need to get to her.

Saint.

Rain soaks my clothes, my hair, my face. My arms shake violently as I pull myself out of the grave and flop onto my stomach.

The words are hoarse from my dry, aching throat. "I'm coming for you, muse."

From my grave, I crawl to her.

CHAPTER TWENTY-EIGHT
BRIAR

SOMEONE IS SHAKING ME AWAKE.

Even before I open my eyes, I shrink away, convinced Trevor is on top of me and calling my name.

But it's not his hands on me. It's not his voice pleading my name over and over.

Saint's mud-streaked face fills my vision. His dark hair is soaked, dripping through the dirt marring his forehead and cheeks. Smoke billows toward us above his head. The manor groans and the front doors crack as the fire roars.

"Saint?"

When he hears the whisper and spots my open eyes, he grabs my hand and sobs against it, shoulders shaking. "Fuck. *Briar.*"

I swallow down the pain, a sob building in my own chest. "I'm . . . I'm sorry."

Sorry I doubted him. Sorry I believed him capable of betraying me, hurting me, of loving anyone else more than he loves me.

"Don't be," he whispers, clutching my hand as he hunches over me. "I'm sorry I didn't protect you from him."

The smoke burns my eyes, my throat. "You did everything you could. You always have."

He lets out another cry, pressing his forehead against mine until he composes himself, frantic gaze finding the smoke filling the ceiling above our heads.

His arms slip under my body until he slowly stands on shaky legs.

"What did he do to you?" I whisper.

"He buried me. He tried to keep me from you. I would never let him do that." Saint slowly carries me away from the fire, smoke still scorching my lungs and throat.

His arms tremble under my weight, but he doesn't drop me.

Trevor buried him alive. And he still found his way back to me. Kept fighting only to save me.

"I'm so sorry I doubted you." Tears burn my eyes that have nothing to do with the smoke. "I . . . I love you. I'm sorry I couldn't say it sooner. And I swear to god I'm not saying it right now just because I almost died."

Through his tears, he lets out a laugh that's tinged with relief and mania. "I love you too. So fucking much, muse. I'm sorry I let him hurt you. I should've been there to protect you." His voice breaks. "I keep fucking up."

"No. You're the only reason I'm still alive."

He clutches me closer, shuffling for the sunroom and the door that leads us outside, away from the fire consuming his beautiful manor.

The brisk spring air mixed with pouring rain pierces my insides in a new kind of pain. "He knocked me out." Tears slip down my cheeks. "He took Mack."

Saint's inky eyes cloud. "Then we need to go get her."

CHAPTER TWENTY-NINE
SAINT

SHE'S ALIVE.

My muse is still alive and in my arms. I could fall to my knees in reverence to the universe for sparing her.

She loves me. My muse finally said the words out loud. The three words I've long been aching to hear spill from those perfect lips.

Over the torrential downpour, a scream makes every hair on my body stand up.

A scream that reminds me entirely too much of the screams emitted from the men I killed before they took their final breaths.

Briar scrambles out of my arms, desperate to get to Mack before she takes that final breath.

From the woods, a lone, dark figure hobbles for the truck parked near the cemetery.

An unconscious body in his arms.

She managed to escape him at some point. She ran from him again, hid long enough for me to get to Briar. Whether she hurt his leg or he fell in the woods, he somehow still got to her again.

She's not dead. He wouldn't kill her. Not after spending so much time chasing her.

But he's taking her.

And who knows how long she'll survive him.

I limp after him, ignoring the screaming muscles in my legs.

Briar runs past me, even as the smoke still scorches her lungs. "You're not getting away with this, motherfucker!"

Trevor opens the back door and stuffs Mack's motionless body into the backseat.

"Stop!" Briar screams.

But Trevor is already jumping into the driver's seat and swinging the door shut.

He slams on the gas, gravel spitting as he follows the path from the private cemetery to my driveway.

Headlights beam onto my face when I leap into his path.

The engine roars, tires squealing as Trevor speeds right toward me. He's not swerving.

A scream rips from Briar that could shatter glass. "*Saint*!"

Heart stopped in my chest, I freeze in the headlights. Briar will never forgive me if I don't do everything I can to stop him. To save her best friend.

Before the truck rushing toward me can make contact, something barrels into my side.

Shoving me out of the truck's path.

We roll to the soft, wet ground together just as Trevor's truck charges past.

I heave in a breath, heart restarting as I stare up at the rain pouring from the night sky. Until her face appears, blue eyes sparking with terror. Her mahogany hair is soaked, strands sticking to her face.

She saved me. She nearly got herself killed. For me.

"Are you okay?" she shouts, helping me rise to unsteady feet.

I want to wrap her in my arms, drop to my knees in gratitude, but we don't have time for that.

At the retreating red taillights, my jaw clenches, on the verge of snapping. He got away. He fucking got away. Before I could make him pay for what he did to us. To my muse.

He nearly killed her.

He took Mack.

But he won't be able to hide from me forever.

"Come on!" Briar screams. "We need to go after him!"

We limp for our cars in the driveway when a loud pop echoes. The truck veers hard to the left, crashing into the wood-line bordering the mile-long driveway.

The back door of Trevor's truck swings open.

Mack jumps out, aiming a gun at the truck with violently shaking hands as she backs away.

She came to. She realized what was happening, who had her, and took a leap of faith.

"Mack!" Her best friend's name rips from Briar's throat.

But at the front of the truck, the driver's side door swings open.

Trevor stumbles out, bleeding from the head.

CHAPTER THIRTY
BRIAR

THE RAIN AND DARKNESS THREATEN TO OBSCURE MY vision, but nothing can hide the blood oozing from Trevor's head.

He reaches up, fingers coming back bloody. Still processing that Mack shot at him. The bullet must've grazed his scalp.

Too bad it didn't go through his skull. That would've put an end to all of this.

Now he's a zombie stumbling toward us.

His blank, unfeeling eyes widen when they land on Saint. He points at the man I love. "You're supposed to be dead!"

"I was just thinking the same about you." Saint is vibrating with barely contained rage.

One word from me would unleash him.

But Mack was right. If anyone deserves to kill Trevor—James—it's her.

She's still pointing her gun at him.

"You fucking shot me!" he wails.

"My aim's usually better." Her voice shakes as much as her hands, but there's a lethal strength beneath them. I've never been so proud of her.

"Toss me your phone," I call.

"What?" Trevor's wild gaze flies to me.

"Give me your phone!"

"Okay!" He holds one hand up while the other slips into his pocket and tosses the phone to me, where it lands on the ground between us with a wet thud. "There! Okay? Please, just call an ambulance."

I snatch up the phone and retreat until Saint's arm is around me again. "What's the passcode?"

He gasps out the numbers. "6-2-2-5."

The numbers spell out *Mack*.

With trembling hands, I quickly find the video of Trevor and April in his phone and wipe it from existence. I won't let him victimize another woman again.

Now we can finish this. "Kill him, Mack."

The torrential rain soaks us all to the bone, mixing with the blood traveling down Trevor's face. He freezes, gaze glued to Mack.

But she doesn't pull the trigger again.

Panic makes my heart skip. She did say she wasn't sure she could kill. Maybe, even after everything he's put her through, she can't bring herself to end Trevor's pathetic life.

The side of his mouth lifts in an arrogant smirk. He knows.

He knows she can't bring herself to kill him.

He takes a step toward her.

I nearly throw myself in between them, but Saint stops me. I wouldn't reach them before Trevor would be on Mack again.

"You're better than them, Mack," he croons. "You're not a killer. You're my angel, remember?"

Bile churns in my stomach at his words. "Don't listen to him, Mack! Give Saint the gun! He'll end this."

Mack doesn't even glance in my direction. Paralyzed.

Trevor takes another hobbling step toward her. And another. Holding out his hand for the gun.

Fuck.

Fuck, fuck, fuck—

Saint grabs my hand, squeezing like I'm his anchor. His lifeline. And he's mine.

"This isn't you, baby," Trevor calls. "Hand me the gun."

"I'm not your *baby*." Her voice cuts through the torrential downpour like a knife.

Mack's clothes are plastered to her body. Beneath her sleeves are likely bruises where he pinned her body to his while he dragged her out of Nicholson Manor. What else did he do to her while I was unconscious?

I hope she's the reason he's limping.

"If you kill me, you'll be just as bad as me." He stumbles toward her again. "Worse."

"I'll always be better than you." The pistol shakes in her hands. "No matter how many times I shoot you."

I hold my breath, and Trevor reaches for a gun hidden at his waist.

A loud *pop* and he stops dead in his tracks.

He clutches his side, and when he draws his hands back to examine them, they're already crimson.

"That's for the first time you slapped me."

Another shot.

Trevor's knees hit the ground.

"That's for the first time you punched me."

My tears mix with the rain. Saint's arms wrap around me, still strong despite everything he's been through tonight.

I flinch when another shot fires and Trevor screams.

"That's for the first time you threw me into the wall."

Pop.

"That's for the first time you choked me."

Pop.

Pop.

Pop.

Blood pools in the grass around him, where he lies face down, motionless.

"That's for the last time."

CHAPTER THIRTY-ONE
BRIAR

WITH THREE WITNESSES REPORTING THE SAME STORY AND corroborating physical evidence, the police have no choice but to believe us. No matter how much I'm sure Officer Smith still wants to believe I'm responsible for everything.

When she arrived at the scene, she probably assumed I killed Trevor just like Austin Emmons and Dr. Barrett. But we all had the same story: Mack killed Trevor in self-defense after he struck her in the head and attempted to kidnap her. Physical evidence proved that I never touched Mack's gun or fired it—none of my fingerprints on the weapon or any gun residue on my hands.

Law enforcement dug into Trevor's past and uncovered the reports Mack filed against him that weren't investigated, which only further corroborated our story. They also found all the disturbing evidence on his laptop.

The fire Trevor set to Nicholson Manor meant we had to cancel the writing retreat. Then when the Auburn Institute of Fine Arts decided to hold formal interviews to find someone to replace Dr. Barrett permanently, I put in my resignation. As much as I once loved the Auburn campus, the memories of Trevor and Dr. Barrett have tarnished it.

Besides, Saint was right. I've been guarding my heart my entire life, refusing to go after what I love out of fear. I love books. So I'm going to become a literary agent—*S. T. Nicholson's* literary agent—and get him the best fucking book deal he's ever signed. His next book is going to blow up, and even if it doesn't, he won't care.

As long as he can place a signed copy on my bookshelf.

While Saint is in the shower, I brew Mack a calming, herbal tea. She's been staying with me since that night at Nicholson Manor.

"How are you feeling?" I ask.

She takes the cup of steaming tea from me with a grateful smile. "Paranoid. Anxious."

"It was self-defense, Mack."

She shrugs. "Partly. Maybe if I'd stopped shooting when he fell to his knees."

"He had a gun. He could've reached for it and shot you. All of us. And he deserved it. After all the shit he put you through—"

"Oh, I know. I'm not saying I regret it. I'm just worried about sharing a prison cell with Big Bertha."

"Who's Big Bertha?"

"The giant, terrifying woman who will take massive shits in our cell at two a.m. and shank me."

"You're not going to prison, Mack." Saint strides into the kitchen, dark hair still dripping, shirt unbuttoned to display his chiseled chest and abs.

Butterflies burst from their cocoons in my stomach every time I see him. Along with Mack, he's been staying with me while Nicholson Manor is being repaired. Fortunately, he can afford to hire around-the-clock workers to fix his home as quickly as possible.

He sweeps me up in a kiss, and I smile against his lips.

"How are you so sure?" Mack asks.

"I've taken care of it."

"What's that supposed to mean?" I swear to god, if he did something to make the police shift their suspicions to him instead—

A sharp knock sends him to the front door. Mack and I exchange a look before trailing after him.

Officers Rosario and Smith are on my front porch. Unfortunate déjà vu.

"Officers," Saint greets in his bright, charming voice. The one that convinces people he's not a serial killer.

Officer Smith cuts right to the chase. "We wanted to let you know that Trevor Hobart has become a suspect in the cases of Austin Emmons and Dr. Charles Barrett."

I gape, but beside me, Saint shows no signs of surprise.

"What did you find?" Mack's eyes are wide.

Rosario gives us a tight smile. "We're not at liberty to say. But we found some DNA evidence in his truck linking him to the cases."

That's impossible. They couldn't have found DNA evidence belonging to Austin or Dr. Barrett in Trevor's truck. Unless—

"We wanted to give you a heads up because you'll probably be hearing a lot more about him in the news," Rosario explains.

I nod. "Thank you for warning us."

We're in the clear. I don't know how he did it, but somehow, Saint fulfilled his promise that I wouldn't get locked up for his crimes.

Rosario waves. "Not a problem. You three have a good afternoon."

Smith doesn't follow Rosario back to the cruiser. Great. I brace myself for further accusations.

"I just wanted to . . . apologize." Her lips are pursed like she swallowed a slug. "For my assumptions. It's rare to find someone linked to two completely unconnected victims and that person not be involved."

I don't know if she actually believes I'm innocent or if Rosario put her up to this. As long as whatever Saint did convinces them of Trevor's guilt, I don't really care what Smith thinks about me.

"I . . . understand," I force out. "Thank you for your apology."

With that, she heads for the cruiser.

"Have a great day, Officer!" Mack calls.

I lock the door behind her and whirl on Saint. "What did you do?"

He shrugs, a cocky smile on his lips. "I may have had some DNA evidence to plant in Trevor's truck."

His trophies. He must've kept something from at least one of the victims and planted it. Potentially linking Trevor to both men. Now that the police know Trevor was stalking me, they've established his connections to the men and his motive.

And he's not alive to deny any of it.

"Oh my gosh!" Mack squeals, beaming and throwing her arms around Saint. "You are *brilliant*! I'm going to call Zayden and let him know he doesn't have to be my prison pen pal."

"Big Bertha will be incredibly disappointed."

As soon as Mack skitters off to make her phone call, I kiss Saint. His lips mold perfectly to mine. Made for each other. "When the repairs to Nicholson Manor are finished, I want to move in with you."

Saint smiles, cradling my face with both hands, more tenderly and lovingly than any other man could muster. "I would be delighted to have you, muse."

Saint, Mack, and Mom help me pack up my belongings. Cookie watches us from her perch on the back of the couch with disdain, disturbed by all of the commotion and her belongings being moved.

"You two are welcome to live with us," Saint reminds my mom and my best friend. My family.

"There are plenty of rooms," I add.

Mom smiles. "That's very sweet of you to offer, but I'm very happy in my home. And no offense, but I don't want to live with you." I open my mouth to express my offense, but she adds, "I don't need to know—or hear—what goes on between you two behind closed doors."

"Agreed," Mack chirps. "But Ginger and I will be visiting all the time."

"You better." I grab a heavy box full of books and carry it out to the car.

Parked in front of my house is a familiar black BMW. April locks the car behind her as she marches up my driveway. She always walks like she has somewhere to be and no time to waste on bullshit. She'll be an excellent lawyer.

She nods to my open trunk. "Moving out?"

"Yep. Turns out I have a stalker."

For the first time, an amused smile crosses her lips. "Listen, I'm sorry I suspected you and lowkey stalked you."

"It's okay. I would've done the same thing."

"I'm sure you've heard by now that the police found Austin's DNA in Trevor's truck." She shakes her head. "I can't believe he was stalking you. He could've killed you too."

"Yeah. He almost did."

Saint is the reason I'm still alive. I'll never be able to thank him enough for everything he's done for me.

April folds her arms. "I'm glad he's dead."

"Me too."

No one else's death has made me happier. Mack is safe now. Trevor can't hurt her or stalk me. He's out of our lives for good. We can finally close this chapter and move on.

April lowers her voice. "Did it really go down the way you said?"

If she's asking, she already has her suspicions. "It was . . . mostly self-defense."

"Do I want to know?" She quirks a brow.

"Only if you're really fucked up."

"Then we'll schedule a coffee date and you can tell me all about it."

CHAPTER THIRTY-TWO
SAINT

THE DAY I'VE BEEN WAITING FOR HAS FINALLY ARRIVED—
the day Briar comes home with me. To our home.

If possible, the repairs to Nicholson Manor have made the estate even more radiant. Or maybe it's simply my muse's arrival that has increased its splendor.

We donated most of Briar's furniture, so it takes us no time at all to move the rest of her belongings. Books, clothes, blankets, Cookie's toys. Cecilia's already in tears before we've even moved the final box inside.

Briar rolls her eyes as Mack and Cecilia both hug her with tears streaming down their cheeks. "I'm literally still in the same state. You can visit anytime."

"These are happy tears," Cecilia wails. "I'm so happy for you!"

"Just wait until the wedding," I tease.

Cecilia's eyes widen and Briar plots my murder. "Oh my gosh! Are you two—"

"No, we're not engaged." Briar flips me off behind her head so her mother can't see.

"Soon, though, right?" Mack glances between us.

I smirk in my muse's direction. "If she says yes."

I know exactly when and how I plan to propose. I'm certain when I do, she'll say yes.

Then we'll truly start our lives together.

"Okay." Mack pulls away from Briar, swiping beneath her eyes. "I'm officially leaving so I don't have to help you unpack."

Cecilia gives Briar one final squeeze. "I'll let you two get settled in." When she releases her daughter, my future mother-in-law gives me a warm smile before wrapping me in a tight hug. "I'm so happy for you two."

Briar is misty-eyed while we wave them off. When they're out of sight, she blinks quickly and clears her throat. "Time to bite the bullet. I'm going to call my father."

I don't ask why. Simply accept the hand she holds out to me and allow her to guide me as she ambles toward the cemetery. A prickle of panic tingles along the back of my neck.

"Yes, it's me," Briar says into the phone. "I'm only calling to inform you that I moved. So you can't show up at my old address unannounced again or someone will call the police on you."

We're in front of the wrought iron fence that guards the private cemetery.

Where Trevor attempted to bury me alive.

The unfamiliar ghostly hand of panic wraps around my throat.

I'm back in that early grave, soil sifting and hissing around me. A muffled scream breaking through the feet of dirt above my head. The desperation to claw my way out, to get back to my muse before I lost her forever. Her voice echoing in my head, calling out to me as I failed to protect her from the monster trying to kill her.

But it was Mack screaming. They both made it out alive. We all did.

Briar keeps her voice brusque, formal. "Saint and I will probably be getting married soon. You're welcome to attend the wedding if you want, but I'm only inviting you because I'm a better person than you are. This isn't a permanent invitation into my life, so after the wedding, I want nothing more to do with you. You took Saint's mother from him. To avenge a man who tried to hurt him. Who probably hurt other children. And you hurt my mom. You hurt me. So I'll never bring myself to forgive you. You can accept that, come to the wedding, and stay out of my life. Or you can choose to stay out now, for good. Your choice. Goodbye."

When she hangs up, I swallow the lump in my throat and squeeze her hand. "I'm proud of you."

Her finger traces over the crease between my brows. "What's wrong?" But before I can answer, she registers our surroundings. "Shit. I'm sorry. We don't have to be here."

She doesn't need to hear my thoughts. She can already read my mind. Knows it just as well as her own. Just as I do hers.

"I'm fine. I'm going to walk out here every day and face my fears." I smile at her. "Just like you did."

She wraps her arms around me, squeezing me close. "I hate what he put you through."

"I'd go through all of it again and worse if it meant keeping you."

"Saint?" she murmurs.

"Yes, muse?"

"I love you. I'll never make you question that again."

I pull back, tilting her chin up to meet her bright blue eyes with a smile. "And I love you. More than anything in this world. So. Shall we break in our new home?"

CHAPTER THIRTY-THREE
BRIAR

SAINT WAS RIGHT—OUR GLORIOUS RETREAT DIDN'T HAVE TO end. Now that I'm his literary agent, we both have book deals. When Saint and I first visited the private cemetery near Nicholson Manor, the kernel of inspiration embedded itself in my brain and wouldn't go away until I caved and wrote the first draft in a frenzy.

While our individual books are ramping up for publication, we're co-writing a series of erotic mysteries for fun. When the timing is right, we'll publish them anonymously in matching masks.

A shipment of S.T. Nicholson's author copies sits on the table in the middle of the library, waiting to be opened. But Saint is preoccupied with his head between my legs.

When I cry out, thighs trembling around his head, he hoists me in the air and pins me against the bookshelf. Books fall down around us as he thrusts into me over and over, my echoing cries mixing with his groans and the thud of books against the floor.

We've finally fucked in every room in Nicholson Manor, but the library is still my favorite.

He pounds my pussy relentlessly until we're both tumbling over the edge.

"Saint!" I scream, nails digging into his shoulders.

"I fucking love you, muse," he growls.

I'll never get tired of hearing those words from his mouth.

I'm breathless when he finally sets me down, heart hammering in my throat. After he recovers, straightening his unbuttoned shirt with a smirk, he turns his attention to the box of author copies.

We both grin as he slices the box open and hands the first copy to me.

The cover of *Dressed to Kill* is stunning, emblazoned with the words *#1 New York Times Bestselling Author*.

"Open it," Saint insists, like it's a gift.

Because it is. Nearly the greatest gift he's ever given me, second only to his heart. The book he wrote because of me. About me. For me.

I flip to the dedication page and my heart stops.

To my muse:

I wrote all my books for you, even before I met you. But this one even more so than the rest. Because this is the book in which I ask you to love me forever. To be mine. To say yes.

When I drag my eyes up from the page, vision blurry, he's kneeling in front of me.

A small box open in his hands and a giant smile across his perfect face.

The ring inside glints and steals my breath.

"During our writing retreat, when I left you here alone, I bought this." He swallows around the lump in his throat. "I knew even then I would someday kneel before you to ask the most important question of my life."

Tears are already pouring down my cheeks, heart in my throat. All this time, he's had my engagement ring. He bought it back when I was still in the early days of falling in love with him. Back when I was still so sure I would never get married, let alone marry my stalker. Back when I was sure I'd never take a man's last name. Never let him make me his.

But Saint had already fallen for me. He was so sure that we'd spend the rest of our lives together. That, in time, I would say yes. I would want to become Briar de Haas. I would want to be his. Forever.

"Muse." Saint's hand reaches for mine, squeezing with heart-breaking tenderness. I've never loved him more. "Will you marry me?"

CHAPTER THIRTY-FOUR
SAINT

Four people are in attendance at our wedding. Briar's parents sit in the white chairs in our backyard, on opposite sides of the makeshift aisle lined with black rose petals. To my surprise, Warren accepted Briar's offer to attend our wedding. He did one thing right by her, at least. Even if he's not happy about his daughter marrying me, he knows he can't stop her.

April Emmons perches beside Cecilia. She and Briar have developed a friendship and even a working relationship when my muse needs legal advice regarding publishing contracts. In the only other chair in the yard, the groundskeeper sits with a giant smile on his face. I could've done without inviting him, but Briar insisted.

The grandparents who took the unearned credit for raising me have long since been buried, but I'm certain that somewhere, my mother watches over us with a smile.

Mack bustles from Nicholson Manor in a deep purple gown that reaches the grass. I rush from the altar to meet her, Zayden at my heels.

"What's wrong?" I bark.

Briar must've developed cold feet. We made it to this day, but she can't bring herself to walk down the aisle.

"Nothing, she's ready." Mack's blue eyes light up when they land on my best man at my side. "God, you look so sexy in a suit."

"You look gorgeous in anything." Zayden grins at her.

Mack beams before throwing her arms around him and pulling him down for a kiss. "I have to go so my best friend can marry the love of her life, but after the wedding, you're dancing with me."

He groans as she turns on her heel and races back to the manor. "I don't dance."

"You do with me!" she calls.

I chuckle as we return to our positions at the altar, a white wedding arch adorned with black and red flowers above my head. "You owe me."

Zayden lifts a brow. "For?"

"For introducing you to your future wife."

"Relax. We haven't even discussed marriage." But I recognize that glint in his eyes. The same I saw reflected back in the mirror after I met Briar. When you know you've met your soulmate.

"Do me a favor? Keep your bedroom affairs out of your next novel. I don't need to read that."

"After you subjected me to the fanfiction about you and your bride? Not a chance."

I wink at him. "Not fanfiction. Completely true. Every detail."

Zayden groans until the violinist starts playing a sweet, dulcet tune, and my heart stops.

Mack slowly marches from Nicholson Manor down the aisle. My bride behind her.

I was right—she's even more beautiful in her wedding dress.

Briar beams at me with every step, the veil already tossed back to reveal her gorgeous face. Her blue eyes bright, her skin radiant, her smile wider than I've ever seen.

My eyes mist.

Mack takes her position at the altar as Briar's maid of honor, and Cecilia is already dabbing at her eyes with a tissue.

When Briar reaches the end of the aisle, she takes my hands.

"I told you." I smirk.

She attempts to glower, but she's too happy to erase the smile from her glowing, perfect face. "Told me what?"

"That you would marry me."

Everyone cries through our vows, written for each other. Briar vows to love and cherish me. I vow to protect and adore her for all of my days.

"Until death," I vow. "And then, until I find you again in the afterlife."

Finally, my muse utters the sweetest words. "I do."

EPILOGUE
BRIAR

"Are you home yet? I'm hungry and waiting outside your house."

"Yes, the honeymoon was amazing, thank you for asking."

Saint chuckles from the driver's seat as we climb the mountain to Nicholson Manor. We visited so many countries in Europe, I lost track of every city we stayed in and every quaint small town we visited. All of it remarkable inspiration for our books. I'm sure we'll both be writing in a creative frenzy by tomorrow.

"I also happen to miss my best friend," Mack adds.

"Will Zayden be able to part with you for a few days while you come visit?"

"He's right beside me. You think you're going to be the only one in that manor getting laid?"

Zayden and Mack have basically been attached at the hip since he flew to Maine and they finally met in person. He claims he moved back because he missed America, but we all know he's here for Mack. They're almost as adorable as me and Saint, and my heart floods with joy whenever I see her smile at him. My best friend finally got the happy ending she deserves.

We both have.

As we pull up to the top of the driveway, Mack and Zayden wave to us, covered in the shade provided by the roof above the entrance. Cookie and Ginger both lay on the steps, sprawled out in the sun.

Saint's hand finds mine in my lap, squeezing. "Ready for our next chapter?"

I grin at him. "I can't wait to write it."

"A story co-written by us?" His dark eyes dance. "A better story has never been told."

After he parks, Saint opens my door, extending a hand to me with a grin and helping me to my feet under the warm sun. Nicholson Manor sprawls out before us. Mine forever to share with the man I love. Ours.

"Welcome home, Briar de Haas."

ALSO BY HARMONY WEST

Want more spicy romance? Check out these standalones by Harmony West!

After Violet accidentally kills her best friend, Wes decides to take justice for his sister into his own hands and turn Violet's life into a waking nightmare in If You Dare.

Madalyn is torn between her perfect boyfriend and the suspicious bad boy after an anonymous stalker targets her in Always with You.

While Cassie searches for her missing best friend and starts to fall for her ex, Noelle wakes up a hostage in someone's basement and must outsmart the dangerous, alluring man holding her captive in Captivate Me.

ACKNOWLEDGMENTS

I truly cannot believe *His Sinner* is my *fifth* published book. So many of you have taken a chance on a brand-new indie author whose books you had never heard of before, and I cannot thank you all enough for reading my dark, twisty books. Thank you for your reviews, your posts, your videos, your comments, and your messages telling me how much you love these books and characters. Thank you for telling your friends, family, coworkers, and disinterested husbands about my forbidden love stories. I will never be able to thank all of you enough for enabling me to do what I love for a living. Thank you.

Thank you to my betas for reading early versions of this story and giving such invaluable feedback: Lauren, Jenni, Isabelle, Kelsey, Kira, Jess, Lianne, and Jaymie. I appreciate you all so much!

Special thank you to Lauren and Kelsey for reading and giving such helpful feedback on all my books but especially this duet. You read these books multiple times and they truly wouldn't be what they are without you. I'll never be able to thank you enough for all your help with my books.

Finally, to Alex: thank you for everything you do for me. You help me run my business, you cook with me, you give me massages when my back is aching from hours hunching in front of the computer, and you always manage to make me laugh, even on the hard days. Thank you for every single day you remind me how proud you are of me for pursuing my dream. I'm so grateful for every day I get to spend with you. I love you.

ABOUT THE AUTHOR

Harmony West writes dark forbidden romance. She enjoys her love stories with a side of mystery, twists, and spice.

For updates on Harmony West's latest releases, subscribe to her newsletter at www.harmonywestbooks.com/subscribe or follow her on social media @authorharmonywest.

Printed in Great Britain
by Amazon

47620648R00121